Old pains revealed, old flames rekindled
and the journey that heals them all.

Echoing Calls of The Spirits

M. R. Walton

The Guardian Saga Begins

iUniverse, Inc.
Bloomington

Echoing Calls of The Spirits

iUniverse books may be ordered through booksellers or by contacting:

iUniverse
1663 Liberty Drive
Bloomington, IN 47403
www.iuniverse.com
1-800-Authors (1-800-288-4677)

Because of the dynamic nature of the Internet, any Web addresses or links contained in this book may have changed since publication and may no longer be valid. The views expressed in this work are solely those of the author and do not necessarily reflect the views of the publisher, and the publisher hereby disclaims any responsibility for them.

Any people depicted in stock imagery provided by Thinkstock are models, and such images are being used for illustrative purposes only.

Certain stock imagery © Thinkstock.

ISBN: 978-1-4502-8561-2 (pbk)
ISBN: 978-1-4502-8562-9 (ebk)

Printed in the United States of America

iUniverse rev. date: 1/8/11

Chapter 1

Cole stood on the front deck watching the moon rising, breathing in the crisp mountain air wishing he could recapture his former life or better yet, go back and re-do the last four years differently. However, wishes wouldn't get him anywhere where as the last few days got him further than the wasted years.

Last night he had ran in his Wolf form, letting the miles fly beneath his paws and after an hour of just blind running, he found himself on a rocky overhang overlooking the entire valley. Sitting on the biggest rock he could find, he raised his head to the sky and let out a howl of jubilation, getting several howls and calls in return. When he heard the last one fade away he felt the old loneliness creep over him replacing his joy. The next howl he let out said it all, low and drawn out, it hung in the air getting no answer. Maybe out of respect, maybe because no one knew how to answer him back.

Today Cole had flown in his Eagle form out of sheer joy because he was chosen to assume the Senior Guardian and Deputy position of the people, like his father and grandfather before him. Being highly thought of by Rick and the Tribunal, that he was considered the best person to be the Peace Chief's deputy was a surprise to Cole.

Later he had listened politely to the new position duties and could barely contain his excitement. Besides himself, there were four other Senior Guardians, two men and two women whom he had known since childhood. They had spent a good part of the day sitting around the main office, swapping stories and getting used to having him as their second in command and ribbing him about the headaches he had inherited.

By mid afternoon, Cole felt totally at ease with his co-workers knowing they all had good spirits, dedicated to the job and well trained. Excusing himself when they brought up old war stories from their youth, he realized he needed some time to himself.

Climbing the mountain to a small meadow he never forgot, he shifted to his Golden Eagle. He stood proudly with his arms held out, palms down, and his head thrown back. He could feel the bones of his arms invert as well as his knees as he took on the structural bone frame of an eagle. He felt the feathers slowly emerge through his skin and cover his entire body, save his legs and feet. As his facial features elongated he opened and closed his mouth experimentally until he heard his beak snap close noisily. He gave a short song of excited peeps until he could let out a screech of joy as he finished his shifting.

With strong swift wings, he climbed higher and higher riding the air currants until he reached the summit and landed. Looking down on the distant community he vowed to protect he knew he had finally found his niche in life and he was finally home, where he belonged.

Screeching out his triumph, again he heard answers of shared joy and acceptance echoing up from the valley back to him. Shaking his feathers as he settled on a deadfall tree, he looked to the east and wondered why he was compelled to search the sky there. Then it all came back to him, she was somewhere out there with out him. Crying out sharply he hoped for a different answer and when none came he tried again, broadcasting louder and longer then he ever had before, hoping to reach her.

The lonely cry surprised him, having never broadcasted the deepest secret in his heart and soul until today. His Wolf, his human and the Eagle yearned for his mates and desperately needed her back to make his life complete.

Again, no answer but then he really didn't expect one since everyone he cared about the most were gone. His brothers were off living their lives outside of the community, his father had passed into the land of the spirits only a few months ago, and Clint was gone forever. Clint would have approved of his return and they would have had one hell of a reunion if he had been here. But then again he would not have left in the first place if Clint hadn't died in that rock climbing accident.

Resting his forearms on the porch rail, he forced himself to remember Clint Red Feather. Cole still felt guilty because he had been late for the climb due to Guardian business. He had been the one to find Clint lying at the bottom of the cliff, his neck broken. There was a broken pinion and clamp lying beside him, the rope still attached to his climbing belt.

He had let out such a cry, loud enough to rouse the entire town as it bounced off the cliff and echoed across the valley. His grief made him inconsolable and unreasonable, fighting the medics when they tried to take Clint's body. Once he had been subdued and sedated he began blaming himself for everything, including things that had happened right afterwards. After two days of either beating himself up or simply locking himself in his room refusing to talk about it, he left. He couldn't face Clint's family, his own or the people of the town, knowing they all had blamed him.

He spent four years long years wondering the country taking small jobs when he needed and keeping to himself, slowly working through his pain. Clint had been more then just his best friend; he had been his blood brother since they were eight. His own father swore that they were tighter then true brothers, each knowing what the other was going to do or say at any given moment. Hell, he had seriously dated Clint's little sister and considered part of the Red Wolf family.

It took a long time for him to accept it was just a freak accident that had taken Clint from them. Coming home was the second to last step in his grieving process; the last step was facing Clint's sister, Becca.

He had expected to run into her when he came home but he had learned through the grapevine that she had left half a year after he did, swearing that she would never come back unless she had to. In a small way, it was a relief not having to face her when he first came back but he knew when they eventually did meet again, it was going to be hell.

Pushing away from the rail he sighed sadly, he just hoped the hell was his alone because she didn't need him anymore. He knew he had done the wrong thing by leaving and it had hurt her badly. Some in the community took great pleasure in telling him just how badly while others either ignored him or turned their backs to him. Walking into the house, he just hoped she would give him a chance someday to explain why he had done what he did.

Rebecca dreamed again of her valley but this time she saw it through her human eyes, wearing her ceremonial dress she stood in the center of the soft swaying grass, singing. Suddenly all the light and beauty was gone and she found herself standing in darkness, facing a set of angrily glowing red eyes. The eyes never blinked or looked away, slowly coming towards her, growing larger then life, filling her with an un-named fear and dread.

Hearing the rustling of dried leaves around her, she watched a pitch-black form move behind the eyes though it never took full shape, it was more like a mist hovering, spreading fear and destruction around it.

She stood where she was proudly, refused to move or stop singing, driving the evil back as her voice grew stronger, more determined. Raising her hands to the sky the apparition faded and the meadow slowly returned to its normal beauty.

Seeing another more benevolent mist forming before her, she lowered her hands until they were reaching out to a slowly forming Spirit wolf. It was a great shimmering silver wolf and she felt no fear of it, standing before it singing. Letting the song softly fade she watched as the wolf advanced towards her recognizing it.

As he walked towards her, he looked deep in to her tear filled eyes and blinked his own golden eyes. "Don't cry anymore Becca. I'm finally free and you should be too." It spoke to her heart, smiling gently. "I'll always be with you but you have to move on and stop mourning me." Stopping beside her it turned it's head to look over the valley then back at her sadly. "You have to go home now little sister. There is evil building there and you're the one who has to find it. You are the catalyst of new change and now's the time for it to begin." Turning to leave it looked over his shoulder and nodded his great head whispering gently, "Go home Becca, before it's too late."

Waking with a gasp, tears running down her face she out towards his fading image, whispering. "Don't go Clint."

Cole tossed and turned as the dream washed over him. He found himself sitting precariously on a rock on the highest peak, looking down on the peaceful valley. Feeling a presence beside him he looked to his left and watched as a Wolf stepped out of a misty cloud. He didn't dare move fearing either he would fall off his rock or the wolf would disappear.

The wolf sat beside him staring up at him with knowing eyes. "You can't keep blaming yourself, blood brother and it's time you got over it. You're home now man, and it's time you started living again."

Cole instantly recognized the voice and turned his head to face his friend's Spirit. Swallowing the lump in his throat, he shook his head sadly. "I should have been there."

"It wouldn't have changed a thing except you would be here, like me. The equipment failed through no fault of ours so stop thinking it's you're fault and don't let it blind you to the truth." Putting a large paw on Cole's tense leg, he rose until he was face to face with Cole and nodded. "I'm free but you're not, so just let it go and look ahead. However, look behind too because everything is not as it should be. You have an important job here now and I know you'll help fix the wrongs." Dropping its paw to the ground and backed away. "You'll do what's right and when all is said and done you'll win what's rightfully yours." Before it turned it grinned then ran into the mist not looking back.

"Wait Clint!" Cole yelled as he sat up awake and sweating. "Wait."

Rebecca drove up the mountain's winding road feeling anxious and bone tired. She had left North Dakota early, days early thanks to her insistent dreams. Taking only two days in Arizona when she had agreed to spend at least a week going through old legends, she had left with little to show for it. She had found an obscure word in the story she was translating that was a mix of two languages, both meaning wolf. It was a puzzling story that would take a long time to figure out, when she had the time.

Slipping a disk in to the player, she cranked the volume up to an indecent level and sang with her favorite song, tapping her fingers on the wheel. She loved to listen to the song repeatedly and set the player to loop play. It made her feel as if it was speaking of her heart and how it felt.

Slowing for the sharp hairpin turn just ahead, she caught a flash of dark brown out of the corner of her eye. Seeing the flash suddenly dodge onto the road directly into her path, she slammed on the brakes with both feet, sliding the truck sideways, blocking both narrow lanes.

A lone wolf with matted fur sat no more then ten feet away from the truck, staring coldly at her. She rolled the window down and returned the stare not blinking, unafraid. The wolf slowly stood and took several steps closer looking at her intently with its hackles raised, as it challenged her for the right of way.

Leaning out the window, she curled her lip back, answering the challenge before whispering. "I belong to the clans of Red Wolf and Red Feather. I am Wolf Eagle. Let me pass."

The wolf lowered its eyes before stepping back quickly at hearing her linage, turned and ran towards the trees, tail tucked between its legs.

Rebecca yelled after it before it could have a chance to announce her arrival. "Don't go telling every one I'm home you jackass!" Watching it lower its head in understanding before slipping in to the underbrush she swore under her breath wondering what was up with it.

Taking several minutes to straightening out her truck, she saw that she had stopped only a mere inch from the edge of the cliff and the shale shelf below. Mumbling to herself, she swore to get that idiot's name and personally have a word or two with him for guarding the territory at such a dangerous spot, not to mention pulling such a dangerous stunt. Anyone else would have driven right over the side if they didn't know the road well enough. Maneuvering until she turned in the right direction she blew out a breath of relief, thankful she had only a few more miles before she was home.

Seeing the brown wolf reappear in her rear mirror, she caught its snarling lips and waved a finger out the window at him as she spun her tires sending gravel shooting back at him. Hearing a surprised yelp when it didn't dodge fast enough she laughed at the sense of justice she had inflicted.

Stopping her truck at the side of the road under the huge leaning pine just above the town, she stepped out to get her first look of her home in four years. Breathing in the clean air deep in to her lungs, she raised her hands above her head stretching her stiff back muscles. Seeing the town spread out beneath her lead her thoughts to the people who lived here.

The people called themselves the Shifting Mountain People, a tribe that was believed to have settled in this valley around the same time as the first people came over the frozen tundra of the Eastern continent. Even then, the people had the unique ability to change or shift into the animals of the totem clans.

Almost everyone here had the gift of a totem spirit residing inside him or her, if not two. The ability to change from her human form to that of either a wolf or eagle was a precious gift from the spirits. Few of her people could do two spirits and there was the rare instance of someone being able to change into a third spirit form. However, it was common that a person who did have three spirits had great difficulty in changing in to that third spirit though they had the senses and strength of that spirit. One spirit residing in a person was considered normal in their community.

She suddenly had the urge to change but hesitated knowing she wouldn't get to her grandfathers until late. As it was, she could see the shadows stretching across the valley signaling evening was fast approaching. Later when she was settled and had time to herself, she would try to feel the air around her but now she had better finish the last leg of her long journey.

Easing the truck back on to the road she didn't notice the recently widened side lane, the soft lights illuminating the log A-frame house or the man standing on the deck watching her as he leaned over the porch rail. Her mind was on the long overdue homecoming and her family's reaction when she knocked on the door.

Finally pulling into the circular driveway, she sighed happy to see nothing drastic had changed; it was as if time had stopped. Leaning back and closing her eyes warily, she let the peace of home recharge her as it soaked in before going on. Hearing a loud piercing whistle, she almost jumped out of her skin and turned to see her grandfather coming around the house pointing his long walking stick at her.

"Looks like you succeeded in sneak in again Child." He growled as he tossed his stick into the bed of the truck before yanking the door open and pulled her out as he looked down at her frowning. "You look tired."

Looking up at him, she wrinkled her nose. "And you haven't changed at all." Giving him a hug, she sighed deeply closing her eyes and leaned in closer. She had always felt safe in his arms, as if nothing could harm her and he could chase away all the evils in the world. "I'm glad to be home finally."

"So am I." Tightening his arms around her shoulders, he pressed a kiss to the top of her head. "The house doesn't feel the same without your spirits stirring things up around here."

Stepping back, she narrowed her eyes at him. "I'm only here for a visit and the ceremony next week Grandda and don't start laying that old guilt trip on me.

I'm wise to your ways, you old wolf." She knew he could charm the spots off a leopard if he put his mind to it and he was bringing up the old argument about her staying this time around.

He grabbed at her shaking finger growling deeply. "Can't blame an old man from trying." Grinning he released her finger to tap her nose with a gnarled knuckle. Reaching around her quickly with a long arm, he pulled a piece of luggage out of the truck bed.

She automatically reached out a hand to stop him but a sharp glare stopped her cold. She knew better than to argue with him, he would do what he wanted whether she liked it or not. Besides, no one in his or her right mind would argue with the Shaman, especially her.

"I may be aging but I'm not feeble child." He growled low as he stepped around her with a heavy suitcase in each hand. "Grab my stick would you?"

Pulling the stick out and shaking her head she reached in the cab for the garment bag hanging behind the seat. "Stubborn old man." Grumbling under her breath, she shook her head.

"I heard that."

Following him into the house, the smells of dinner and her mother rattling pans inundated her overly sensitive ears. Hearing a pot lid hit the floor she bit her lip to keep from laughing as her mother sensed she was there.

"Rebecca Ann Red Feather, how dare you sneak in?" Her mother scolded as she flew from the kitchen to her daughter, fighting to get her apron untied. "You said in a week or two." Throwing her arms around her baby girl, she laughed and cried at the same time as she rocked her child in welcome.

Rebecca gasped as her mother squeezed her tightly and rained kisses on her head. "Mom, I can't breathe." Mumbling into her mothers shoulder, she struggled to get free.

"Sorry Becca." Regina laughed and released her to look her over critically. "You look so, tired."

"Why does everyone tell me that?" Stepping away, she leaned the stick against the coat rack and shrugged. It was the same every time she came home and she knew what ever she said wouldn't make a difference. "I've been driving for over twelve hours so yeah, I'm a little tired."

"Well go up, drop everything and dinner will be ready shortly." Pushing her daughter towards the stairs, she fussed with Rebecca's hair. "Everything is the way you left it, we haven't changed a thing. And there's fresh linen on the bed."

"I'll only be a minute." Running up the stairs, she passed her grandfather as he was coming down and rolled her eyes. "She's never going to stop seeing me as a little girl, is she?"

"Nope. I see her the same way; it's a fact of life." Shrugging he grinned and patted her on the head. "I hurry up now, I'm hungry."

Ducking into her room at the top of the stairs before he could reprimand her for running, she laid the bag on the foot of the bed beside her luggage. Glancing at herself in the full-length mirror, she groaned in disbelief. Her hair looked a mess; wind blown was putting it mildly. Grabbing the antique silver brush, she quickly worked out the tangles and began pointing out her flaws and her assets.

She was short, only five two and fine boned, smaller and more delicate then most people she knew. Her face was narrow with high cheekbones and a short narrow nose over what she considered a too generous mouth. Her brown eyes showed signs of being tired, light circles made them look more sunk in then they usually were.

She knew she could stand to put on a few pounds but her high metabolism kept her almost rakishly thin. Her breasts were a big disappointment to her because they barely existed. She could get away with out wearing a bra most of the time. She hated to admit it but until she had let her hair grow long, she had been mistaken for a boy more times then she cared to count. It now hung to her knees, straight, fine and jet black and her only good asset as far as she was concerned.

Seeing the old black and white picture hanging on the mirror, she realized she was the exact image of her grandmother. Nana may have been tiny but she had had a dynamic personality and a strong will just like her namesake. She recalled her grandfather saying that 'dynamite came in small packages, nitro came in smaller ones, and they were named Rebecca.' She just wished she could remember her grandmother and Nana was here to see how well her granddaughter had grown up.

Hearing her mother call from the bottom of the stairs breaking in to her thoughts, she quickly secured her hair in a ponytail and went down to join her family for dinner.

Pushing her plate away a half hour later she sighed as she reached for her teacup. "Now that's worth coming home for."

"There's pie if you've got room." Regina raised a delicate eyebrow waving the pie plate before her. "The last of the winter apples."

"Later, maybe. No room." Winking at her grandfather over her cup, she blew at the steam. "I'll raid it later, so don't hide it."

Leaning back, she closed her eyes and missed the look her mother threw at her grandfather. She had expected at least one lecture during dinner but none had been forthcoming and she was going to enjoy the reprieve for as long as she could. She felt the room grow a little tense and suppressed her shudder.

"Dad, why don't you build a fire, it's still a little chilly. I'll get this cleaned up while you and Becca catch up on what's been going on around here."

Rebecca opened her eyes to see her mother nod towards the living room and knew there was going to be bad news and she was involved by the way her mother avoided looking at her. Pushing away from the table, she picked up her plate.

"Not tonight, just relax and enjoy the break." Regina shook her head taking the plate from her daughter's hand. "Go on."

Sitting on the sofa in front of the huge fireplace, she watched her grandfather start a fire. "What is Mom not trying to say?"

"Oh, she's just rattling." He grinned over his shoulder as he stuck another piece of wood into the building flames. "You know her."

Watching him wince as he stood she narrowed her eyes trying to read his body language. "What is she hiding?"

Leaning on the mantel, he sighed as the heat soaked into his sore knee joints. "I'm getting old. My joints hurt worse every year."

"Now you're rattling Grandda. Might as well get it out in the open." Staring at him, she watched as he picked up a familiar picture frame and turned her head hiding her discomfort. "I thought you would have gotten rid of that picture by now."

She knew that picture well; it had been on of her favorite's way back then. Cole and she were smiling for the camera; he was standing behind her, his arms around her shoulders possessively. They looked so happy back then and so in love. "I wish you would just burn that."

"You two were right for each other." Max replaced the picture and sighed. "It's hard to believe it ended like it did."

Setting her cup on the end table, she shrugged. "And there's nothing that can turn back the clock, so why bring it up?"

Turning he stood against the mantel. "Hey, we've had a number of returns this year." Pushing himself from the heat he walked to her and sat beside her taking her hand. "We now have members of the Owl clan here and more of the Bear clans."

Watching him playing with her fingers, she sighed. "And?"

"Cole Sun Wolf came home a few months ago."

Her head shot up and searched his weathered face. "He came home?"

Despite the roaring fire, she felt a chill run through her and shivered. "He's got guts, I'll give him that." Trying to pull her hand free she saw his scowl.

"He had nothing to do with Clint's death and you know it in your heart, don't you?"

"I know but that's not the issue. It's what he did afterwards that makes me hate him." Jerking her hand free she stood and walked stiffly to the bay window. "He didn't even wait to bury his friend or say good-bye to me! He just ran away."

"Honey, he blamed himself and couldn't face you." Max whispered to her stiff back. "He still feels guilty."

"And I'm supposed to welcome him back, letting it all go? I don't think so because I still hate him and my forgiveness isn't in the cards." Hugging herself, she looked to the ceiling. This was the reason she hadn't been home in over a year, they never failed to bring him up and she just didn't want to talk about it. "He hurt me so deep and he dishonored Clint." Whispering to herself, she wiped away a tear. "It's unforgivable."

"He deserves a chance to explain to you, in person. He is a changed man, so full of grief and emptiness. He's a lone wolf now, Becca." Her mother whispered as she joined the conversation and stood behind her.

"Well you can just tell him to stay the hell away from me. I don't ever want to lay eyes on him nor do I want to hear anything from him as long as I live." Turning to her grandfather, she held up her hand to silence him. "He's a coward as far as I'm concerned."

"He's no coward!" Max stalked across the room to tower over her and cupped her face with not too gentle hands. "Cowards never return to their people or face their demons like he has." Silently pleading he held out his hand to her retreating back.

Running from the room, she paused half way up the steps before laughing coldly. "You couldn't prove it by me."

Lying on her bed, she stared at the wall letting the anger, bitterness and loss boil inside her. She thought about

Cole and her misplaced hope of finding him as her true mate. But the day her older brother died from a fall rock climbing, Cole tucked tail and ran. He had left her grieving, not saying a word when she needed his support the most. When the rumors started flying Rebecca took none of it to heart, disbelieving the worse of Cole Sun Wolf. 'He's been in trouble with the Guardians ever since he was five years old and it's not surprising he was some how involved in the accident. What really made her start to believe part of the rumors and whispers were the fact that Cole never returned to defend himself or tried to talk to her.

After only six weeks the investigation of Clint's death wrapped up and everyone was surprised to learn it was ruled an accidental death. According to the Chief Peace Officer, Clint's equipment was improperly maintained and deemed at fault. Rebecca knew then in her heart, Cole could not have been involved. Clint had been Cole's best friend and they were blood brothers since early childhood.

To this day, she couldn't get past the fact that he had left her with out a word, sneaking out of town in the middle of the night like a thief. She had made an oath to never trust another man or let one in her heart that easily again. It was just too painful a lesson learned.

When she finally had enough of those feelings, she slipped from her room and the house without speaking to her family. Sitting on the back deck for several hours, she watched the stars, searching for help to shrug off the blanket of pain and give her some peace. The only thing the night sky gave her was a beautiful display of the aurora dancing down from the north in slow hypnotic waves but no reprieve.

Rubbing her chilled arms, she thought she saw movement out the corner of her eye, a flash of silver and it was gone. Jumping to her feet she ran to the side rail as she saw another flash headed north through the trees. She waited for several heartbeats but didn't see it again. Shrugging she went back in and up to her room on tiptoe so she wouldn't wake her now sleeping family.

Sitting at the writing desk, she turned on the small desk lamp and opened the bottom drawer. Pulling out the old photo album she ran her hand over it but laid it aside, not ready to look at her memories. Finding what she was looking for she pulled out the stack of letters, all from Cole. Each one was from somewhere different and about a month apart. Adding these to the stack on the edge of the desk, she counted forty-six letters in all. They were all unopened and she simply held them in front of her. She couldn't imagine what they said but she wasn't ready to find out.

Dropping them back in to their prison, she closed the drawer and sighed. One day maybe she would have the courage to read them but not in the near future. She wanted to keep that knife from twisting again, cutting out the last remaining piece of her poor heart. Turning off the light she undressed and finally crawled under the sheets to drop into a deep sleep.

Cole felt restless and the tension made his neck hurt which kept him from sleeping. He knew before anyone had to tell him that she was home. He had seen her when she had taken that small break at the end of his drive and he had almost approached her but something held him back.

Watching her stretch he had caught his breath, she hadn't changed much in four years. Her hair was longer and she looked a lot thinner then he remembered, more delicate but knew she was stronger than everyone assumed. He felt the tightening of his stomach and his spirits stir restlessly as she left, not seeing him on the deck.

Pacing the dark, he faced the fact that they would come face to face sooner then he expected and he was sure it was not going to be pretty.

He watched a dim light go on then off a short time later in the Red Wolf house and knew she was there across the valley but yet a world away. He also knew that she never replied to his letters but she hadn't sent them back either, his heart whispered. There was still a small glimmer of hope burning inside but as time went by that glimmer had begun to fade away.

Clint had told him to let the past go and to look forward, so that was what he would try to do.

Thinking on that dream, he felt he had missed something important but could not put his finger on it. Clint had tried to tell him something but he had missed it. Feeling frustrated when he couldn't get it he pounded on the railing.

"Damn it Clint, why couldn't you just come out with it?" He growled into the night as he pushed away from the railing. "Why be so damn cryptic?" Yelling out his frustration into the darkness, he stomped into the house and slammed the door behind him.

He didn't notice the pair of glowing red wolf eyes watching him closely from the woods nor did he hear the low growl over his shouts.

The next day Rebecca helped with the preparations for the mid summer celebration ignoring her families worried glances. Rebecca thought mostly of the other members of the Shifting Mountain People. They were like no other People, they could boast of being unknown to outsiders for over four centuries. They knew before the first European had come to this land that things were about to change and the people had just disappeared, spreading out in every direction.

Most had lost their way in the world, until about a century ago when a small band gathered together to take jobs as miners in the near by mine. They built the town with the wages earned and began calling their brothers' home, to Indian Mound, Idaho every year at this time with the knowledge that the outsiders would eventually leave. Many of the Shifters did come home bringing with them new blood lines tracing back to the beginning of time. It wasn't uncommon now to carry a Native American name but have blond hair and blue eyes or visa versa, but all were welcomed home as long lost children.

They still live in the community deep in the Sawtooth Mountains as far from the old mining towns as they could with out being reclusive. Yet they were not so far removed that they didn't have all the modern conveniences. Fortunately with so many Shifting Mountain people living here they were actually now living on a Federally designated reservation.

Becca worked hard from sunrise to well after the moon set all the while laughing with her friends and meeting the new arrivals as she helped out. Everyone was excited to learn she was home for an extended visit this time instead of only day or two like she had done in the last four years. Occasionally she felt eyes watching closely her every move but she couldn't figure out who was staring holes in her back. It wasn't a scary or disturbing feeling but it did make her nervous at times.

When she caught a glimpse of Cole Sun Wolf walking up the steps to the Council building she froze mid-step. At this distance he looked like he hadn't changed much from what she remembered, his hair was longer and he seemed bigger some how though there was a dim darker aura around him now.

She realized Pris Cool Rain was standing at her side, watching her closely and she suppressed her shudder. "I heard he was back."

"Yeah and keeping to himself. I know many of the females between sixteen and sixty are trying to get his attention. The funny thing is half of the women are already married." Pris whispered under her breath, nudging her arm. "He just blows every one of them off and I personally think he still has a thing for you."

Rebecca narrowed her eyes and gritted her teeth as she seethed inside. "I am not interested, not now or in the future. And you can drop that little tidbit in the gossips ears for all I care." She was sick and tired with everyone throwing Cole up in her face. Turning to face Pris, she sneered. "I wouldn't give him the time of day if he was the last man on Mothers land." Throwing up her hands, she stomped away leaving her friend standing there, mouth-hanging open.

Cole saw Rebecca running around town and considered approaching her several times but she seemed to keep people around her as a living shield. He had already heard the old grannies gossiping about her, her visit home and he wisely ignored them. The only thing he took away from their gossip was that Becca was still unmarried and she had made a name for herself out in the world. He did not know if that was good or bad, by the way they cackled watching her from across the commons.

He caught her silvery laugh on the breeze many times, each one making him stop to listen soaking them in. He tried to look inconspicuous as he kept up with her to hear more but when he got close to her, she was on the move again.

Checking his watch, he circled the commons once more before heading to the Guardians office to get his daily duties done. Picking up his pace, he politely nodded to another group of grannies on a shaded bench, stumbling when he heard her laugh float in the air again.

Just as he opened the door to the council building, he felt her eyes on his back and felt the sharp daggers almost as if they were real. Bowing his head, he turned his head slightly, saw her glaring at him, and knew she would never approach him or let him approach her openly. Stepping in to the building he suddenly decided that he would just have to confront her whether she liked it or not. Avoiding the inevitable was only going to make things worse.

After going over the next month's duty roaster until his head felt like it was going to explode, he decided it was good enough to lay on the boss's desk for his signature. Stopping at the snack machine, he heard the phone ring and one of the other guardians picked it up. Punching in his selection, he heard Mike yelling for him and groaned. He really didn't want to go out on a call this late in the shift but he knew everyone else was out or coming in later.

"Yeah, what's up?" Walking down the hall, he tore into the bag of chips and poured some into his hand. "What do you got?"

"Some one just called in saying there's kids acting really strange down on the commons. She says she thinks they're smoking weed and saw a couple popping pills."

"Where's this happening?" Dropping the chips on the desk, he grabbed the report and cleared his throat. "Did she say who she was?" Looking at the complainant name block, he saw it was blank and frowned.

"Sorry." Mike grabbed the paper and quickly scribbled a name then handed it back to him. "She said she was

Rebecca Red Feather, and she's over by the drinking fountain pay phone."

"Okay, I'll take it. Tell Rick to get ready for another long night." Pocketing the paper, he grabbed his Baseball cap and waved as he stepped out the door. Checking to make sure his side arm was strapped securely in the holster resting on his hip and he pulled his badge out from under his shirt, he pushed the main door open and took a deep breath.

He could see her from here, pacing the sidewalk in front of the phone, twirling her hair between her fingers and throwing dark looks at the kids as they started messing around and on the newly carved totem poles.

Dodging across the street he watched the kids and clamped his lips closed when he saw one openly light up a joint. Sneaking a glance at Becca he saw her scowl and stomp her foot when the pay phone rang. When he saw one of the older kids run to the phone almost knocking Becca over, he had enough. Running up he held out his badge and whistled to get their attention as he stood before them.

"Guess what guys, you're all under arrest." Grinning he gave them a big toothy smile, and then narrowed his eyes recognizing a few of them. Grabbing the first runner, he laughed and shook his finger at the others. "And if you run, you're in bigger trouble. So just step on down and let's go for a little walk." Pushing the runner in front of him, he nodded to Becca as she stood off to the side, watching with a look of smug satisfaction on her face. "I'll be back."

Herding the kids to the Guardians office and the waiting cells, he laughed when they began to spit out their conflicting stories. "Look, you're going to shut up and wait till your folks come. Then you can tell us what the hell you thought you were doing. Until then sit down, shut up and think of what your parents are going to do to you when they get here."

Shaking his head, he closed the cell doors and took a deep breath to keep from laughing. They thought they were in trouble for messing around the poles and in the fountain and he figured if they sat for a little while it would not hurt. Handing a list of the names he asked Mike to start calling parents and ask them to come in and claim their kids. "I'll be right back, need to get Becca's statement."

"She said that she wouldn't come in when she called back. She said the officer should've seen enough that her statement wasn't needed." Mike shrugged. "She sounded a little ticked and hung up on me when I tried to tell her she still needed to come in."

"Yeah, well she's probably scared. But I'll see if I can convince her." Straighten his hat he grinned. "I can lay on the charm and she'll be ready to come in."

"If she doesn't rip your head off, first," Mike warned. "I know who she is, took me a minute but I remember."

"So do I, believe me." Sighing he pushed the door open and steeled himself for an ugly scene.

Becca searched the sidewalk around the fountain and the grass near the totem poles and found several lighters along with a few small parts of joints floating in the fountain. Shaking her head, she wondered when and how drugs found their way into Indian Mound. Hearing footsteps behind her, she felt him coming towards her and took a deep breath.

"Becca?' his voice was the same, rich and deep. "I have to get a statement from you."

"I told the officer who took my call that the Guardians didn't need it because you saw them." Keeping her back to him, she waved her hand at the fountain. "There's enough evidence to make the arrest stick, so you don't need me." Turning slightly she glared at him. "Just like before."

"Don't do this Becca, it wasn't like that." Reaching out to her, he stopped and closed his hand when she narrowed her eyes. "Please?"

"Go away Cole, I don't want to talk to you and I sure as hell don't want to look at you." Waving him off, she ran from him before he could say another word.

Chewing the inside of her cheek, she kept her mumbles to herself until she was well away from him. "I hope you fall in and crack your skull."

Cole watched her stiff back as it disappeared behind the willow trees and looked around to see if anyone had witnessed their first meeting. Relieved to see everyone too engrossed in their work instead of the brief confrontation between him and Becca, he hung his head. Working his jaw, he cursed himself out for not being a little nicer and maybe a little more professional.

Stepping into the cold water, he scooped up the few roaches floating there and shook his head when he saw a little zip lock baggie lying under the water. Picking it up gingerly, he groaned when he saw a white rock. "Son of a buck toothed beaver." Kicking the water, he let his anger loose for an instant. Pot and crack cocaine in the hands of the kids meant that the bust was beyond a simple slap on the hand from parents. This time it meant juvenile time for most of them and another lecture from the Tribunal. Unfortunately, somehow the garbage was still getting into the community and in the hands of kids who didn't know better.

Chapter 2

At the end of her exhausting day Rebecca climbed up the front steps pleased that she had survived it without having a total meltdown. All day she had heard about how great Cole was, how available and how he was such a good-looking man. The only time she had let her control slip was when she had been snide with Pris. She regretted it but she could not hide the fact that she really did not give a hoot about him anymore. Then to have to talk to him about the kids and the drugs, it just made her mood worse.

She had tried to avoid anyone who even looked like they were going to bring him up during the potluck. She had to struggle to keep herself civil and now she was paying for it dearly. Her head pounded as if there was a jackhammer trying to make its way out, taking the long way. Her shoulders felt like she had carried the new totem pole down from the mountain all by herself after chiseling it with a butter knife.

Stepping on to the porch, she saw a small white rose propped against the door and stopped before it. Looking around she knelt and picked it up with two fingers mindful of possible thorns. Turning it gently she saw that it glowed in the soft porch light, giving off a sweet scent as she brought it to her nose. Feeling something scratch her nose, she stood and found the small slip of paper tucked between the petals. Pulling it out she glanced around again before she carefully unrolled it.

She didn't recognize the practiced elegant writing, which held her interest but only for a moment. Reading the single line her brows drew together and she threw the note and the rose away from her as if they burnt her fingers.

Wiping her hands on her jeans, she gave a shudder as she opened the door. Glancing around nervously she saw nothing in the waning light as she stepped into the house and kicked the door closed behind her, muttering to herself. How dare he try this, especially when she point blankly told him to leave her alone.

That night she dreamt that she was standing in the center of a valley similar to the one above her family's home as she cocked her head to the side, paying closer attention to the chorus of calls. It was the annual return home call but what she noticed was mixed with it was a low lonesome, vaguely familiar voice. She felt that call more then heard it as it overrode the chorus of the others, it pulled at her heart with a strength and intensity that was new to her. It carried notes of sorrow, desperation and intense emptiness.

It almost made her call back but something in the back of her mind stopped her from raising her head and voice to the wind. She didn't know if it was just the uncertainty in her mind or some long forgotten fear she had buried deep inside that stopped her. She followed the call cautiously, curious as to who or what had caught her attention. Walking slowly towards the west she thought she heard the call of 'where are you?' leading her to new unexplored territory far off in the distance, well after the others calling faded.

Groaning she unburied her head from under the pillows, still feeling the unsettling pull of her heart. When the call faded to an echo filling the empty niche in the furthest corner of her mind with the rest of her dreams, she shuddered as the echo continued.

The note fluttered off the porch and then floated on the light breeze, landing some yards away. In the shadows Cole bent and picked it up, crumpling it in his long fingers, so much for being subtle and nice, he thought as the rose's scent reached him from the bottom of the porch steps.

He had kept to the shadows and avoided everyone during the impromptu potluck, his eyes never leaving Becca. He wondered if anyone else noticed that she was laughing a little too hard and loudly at the jokes towards the end of the evening. He had watched her put on her best smile but he knew it was as phony and forced, as was her laugh. He also saw her when she was not surrounded by people, threading a thin braid through her fingers. Her slight frame seemed to shrink in on itself, almost as if she was trying to become invisible.

He had left when she began easing away from the crowd hoping to catch her before she could make good her escape. After snitching the rose from Mrs. Dearborn's garden, he headed for her house and waited for her. After what seemed like hours, he decided to leave a note with the rose and carefully wrote 'I'm sorry' in the porch light. It did not seem like a lot but it was the truth.

He had just reached the shadows when he heard her approach and waited behind the bushes to see her response. Seeing her throw his peace offering away he knew then he was going to have to change his tactics if he wanted to get close enough to talk to her.

The next day Cole felt as if he was being called up to the attic and went reluctantly, up to the hall of memories as his father used to call it. He found boxes that held toys and photo albums, spanning many generations but had to remind himself that these were not his mission today.

What he wanted was sitting by itself, covered in a light dust in a ray of sunshine in an otherwise gloomy room, almost calling to him. Ducking beneath the sloping rafters, he pulled it closer with shaking hands. Kneeling he pulled off the lid and took a deep breath as he looked inside.

Seeing his climbing gear and a carefully wound rope lying on top he groaned as it hit him hard. He knew his father had taken no joy in packing this all up after he had left.

Pulling the rope out, he gave it a good tug at several intervals and checked the knots. Laying it aside, he noticed the clamps lay out as if waiting for him to put them to work once again. Looking them over carefully he noticed what looked like scratches marring the surface of one of them.

Bringing the clamp up to his eyes he realized the scratches around the ring were too deep and not from normal wear and usage. Picking up the other clamp, he saw the slip ring was damaged too. There was a deep grove in the inner metal that looked like someone had been filing away at it. Dropping his hands, he closed his eyes and gave a deep groan, if he had used them he would have been in serious trouble. Laying the clamps to his right he pulled out a pair of spikes used to set into rock cracks. The spikes were cracked and one had a v cut into it making them just as unsafe as the rings and clamps.

He felt chills run up his back to the roots of his hair. He was supposed to climb with Clint that day. Pulling the rope closer he ran his fingers over the entire length looking for defects, finding none he dropped it to his left. Digging deeper into the box he found his harness carefully folded. He knew it was in excellent shape having used it only once since he bought it. Running it through his fingers, he felt nothing until he reached the buckle. The over lap seam was barely holding and when he tested it with a good tug the buckle came off.

The hair on the back of his neck stood straight up when he heard Clint's deep voice in the back of his mind. 'The equipment failure was no fault of ours', echoed in his head. "Damn it."

Scooping up the clamps, d-rings and harness he ran down the stairs and out to his truck heading for town.

Skidding to a stop in front of the building, he continued his one word litany and beat against the steering wheel. Throwing open the door he scooped everything up and stomped into the building, ignoring the startled glances of people as he passed them.

Seeing the stunned looks on everyone's face in the office as he burst through the door, he clamped his mouth tight and headed straight for Rick Running Waters office. Entering without knocking he knew he had just broke Rick's number one rule but didn't give a damn. "I need some help Rick." Growling he tossed the equipment on his bosses already cluttered desk, scattering papers everywhere. "I need to know if all of this is what I think it is."

Rick looked at the gear then up to Cole. "It's climbing gear." Picking up the harness, he shrugged. "Good quality stuff if I know my gear."

Cole leaned over the desk and jabbed his finger at the buckle strap. "New stuff does not fall apart after one use and its brand spanking new!"

"Who's is this?" Glancing up he noticed Cole's usually calm golden brown eyes were black and hard. "All of this is yours?"

"Yeah, mine. I want all of this stuff checked out because this really stinks of tampering." Grabbing a ring, he pointed out the odd scratches. "This is not normal."

Rick peered at the ring grunting. Seeing the uniform scratches he had to admit Cole was right. "I'll send this stuff to a friend of mine who's with forensics. I'll see if he can take a look right away and tell us if it's normal or not."

Pacing Cole nodded and finally dropped into the chair behind him. Running his fingers through his hair, he laid his head back and sighed. He couldn't find an easy way to bring up the thoughts running through his head, so he just blurted out his dream about Clint's veiled hint. When he finished he was hunched over, his folded hands dangling between his knees. "I think he was telling me his death was no accident and I was targeted too."

Rick sat back in his chair and watched Cole closely through hooded eyes. "You know the results of Hanks and the coroners report as well as anyone."

"Yeah, they said equipment failure." Looking up he snarled. "Who actually investigated and just how well did they check Clint's gear?" Taking a deep breath, he picked up the harness. "Clint used the same gear I did and we bought our harnesses at the same time, at the same place."

Rick leaned across his desk scowling as he got the drift of what Cole was saying. "I know you two were blood brothers and all but this sounds too incredible." Seeing the younger man's eyes narrow, he threw up his hand. "Okay, I'll send Clint's gear along if it'll make you feel any better. It is still in the property room because his family never claimed it. But don't get your hopes up." Sitting back, he rubbed his jaw slowly. "And this is between us because if his family catches wind of this they're going to freak."

"Clint said I would do what's right and in the end I would win."

Rick shook his head and folded his hands on the desk. "I don't know about Clint talking to you but I can't argue against it." He never experienced a visitation but he could not discredit Cole's story. "I'll send this out in the morning but for Gods sake, don't go stirring any crap. You are still considered somewhat of a pariah by some folks. So don't give them any more ammo."

Cole gave a bark of laughter as he tossed his head back. "I've been the people's black sheep since I was five. They're gossip doesn't bother me anymore." Shrugging his shoulder he let the advice roll off him. "But I hear ya." Standing he held out his hand to Rick, who immediately took it. "I'll keep my nose clean."

Rick nodded as he grinned. "You sure don't look like the big bad wolf that terrorized the town."

"The only ones who feared me were the protective papa's and momma's and they where the ones who considered me a wolf." Grinning he raised an eyebrow and added. "Though I never deserved it, trust me."

Rick shook his head and pointed to the door. "Yeah right, it's your story." He realized he had made the right choice in promoting Cole up to his deputy. The man had the ability to turn a tense situation in to a calm one when needed. "Get out of here."

Leaving the office only feeling slightly better Cole buried his anger long enough for him to reach his truck. Sitting behind the wheel, he found new determination to find out what really happened to Clint that day and changed everyone's lives. He would re-open the case and find the truth, even if it killed him.

Rebecca shifted her feet uneasily on the low stool, her arms held out at her shoulders while her mother slowly circled her tapping a finger on her cheek. "Mom, can I please put my arms down?"

"No. I can't figure out what is wrong with this dress if I can't see the whole effect."

"I'm melting, my arms are sore and the dress is perfect." Rolling her eyes, she felt the stool wobble precariously. "I'm done." Dropping her arms, she jumped off the stool before she fell off.

"I've got it!" Regina took her daughters shoulders and swung her around in a slow circle. "The fringe is missing from the sleeves. Dad said the sleeves should move even after you stop moving." Holding out one of Rebecca's arms, she nodded. "They are supposed to hang from your elbow to your knees."

"Fine, have Grandda put them on later, right now I want to take this off before I sweat to death and I want food." Hearing her stomach attest to her hunger, she pulled her arm free. "See?"

"All right, all right, Get changed, you bear." Helping, she held the dress up as Rebecca slipped out from under it. "Dad should have it fixed quick enough."

"I still think it's perfect as it is," Grumbling she stepped around the bed to the open window. "But I'm not going to argue about it."

"All right, what's wrong?" Laying the dress across the bed Regina stood before her daughter, her hands on her hips. "You're wound tighter then a clock and grumpier then a bear after hibernation."

Rebecca pulled back from her mother's glare and snatched up her discarded t-shirt. "I got overwhelmed by people yesterday telling me all about Cole and how great he is." Turning she scowled at the window. "I don't care and they keep bringing him up."

"You know he would come up in conversation sooner or later. Everyone expected you two to make the claiming and marry some day." Sitting on the stool Regina watched her daughters back stiffen. "And I expected grandchildren by now."

"I just wish they would drop the subject before they drive me completely nuts." Rubbing her aching temples, she paced the floor.

Sensing something else bothering her daughter she patted her knee and cocked her head. "Come cuddle with me for a minute."

Sitting on the floor, Rebecca scooted close to her mother and laid her head on her knees. "I miss this."

"I do too." Caressing her daughter's hair, she gave a quiet sigh. She decided to wait before broaching the subject of Rebecca's real problem. "I've got a new story for you. Has anyone said anything to you about Miles Darkwing and Martha since you came back?"

Closing her eyes, she surrendered to her mothers calming touch. "No but I'm sure you are going tell me."

"Apparently he's been harassing the woman folk, cornering them in the market, following them around town or just drop by their homes at odd times. For a while, everyone just thought that he was lonely but then it got worse and a few of the younger ones have begun to complain. They say he practically stalks them now until they threaten him with bodily harm." Pulling the hair from Rebecca's face, she chuckled. "Anyway, Martha got fed up with him following her around town, dogging her every move. One day she finally had enough and changed into her bear, chasing him across the commons. Everyone who witnessed it swore up and down that he left a trail all the way to his front door."

Rebecca covered her mouth when she started to laugh, seeing it in her mind as Regina continued. "He doesn't distinguish between single or married women anymore. And he learned the hard way to not mess with a married new mother."

"She really chased him?" Gasping she tried to catch her breath. "I'm surprise Allen didn't call Miles out over that." Allen was a jealous and protective man with a strong belief that all women are to be treated with honor and respect.

"Oh Allen's mellowed a bit. He said that if Martha can handle Miles she can protect herself and the babies as a big ticked off grizzly any time." She chuckled as she shifted a little. "She only has to roar now and Mile's wets himself."

Rebecca laughed until she cried. Wiping the tears away, she hugged her mothers' legs and began shaking as her tears continued. In a shaky breath, she slowly told her mother about the dreams she had been having. She gave the details about the terrifying eyes and the black form behind it in a small voice like a frightened child. When she finished she was shaking like a leaf. "Mom, I'm scared."

"Oh honey, so am I." Rubbing her daughters taunt back, she rocked back and forth. "Is that why you came home Becca, to warn us that something's going to happen?"

"Partially for that reason. The other reason is that I have been gone for four years and need to get centered." Shrugging she took a deep breath. "I need some peace but I don't think I'm going to get it any time soon."

"Well we'll see what happens." Patting the slowly relaxing back, she closed her eyes. "I'll talk to Grandda on your behalf, if you want me to."

"No. I'll do it, it's my problem." Sitting up she wiped the tears from her face. "But give me a day or two in case it comes back clearer."

"Okay, but you've got two days or I'll tell him." Moving to stand she hoped her daughter's precognitive dream did not foretell exposure of their people. "Let's get you something to eat."

Heading down the stairs they both jumped when they heard a loud bang against the front door. Rebecca flew down the stairs passing her mother and yanked the rattling door open to find a large cougar leaning against it. The animal was bleeding heavily from the snout and mouth, gasping for air.

It barely had enough energy to hold itself against the doorframe when it gave a gasping breath and slowly collapsed. Falling across the threshold at Rebecca's feet it growled low in its throat before losing consciousness.

"Sweet Gods, its Christophe Running Waters." Regina rushed to the fallen animal and watched as it slowly changed to a nude young man. "Christophe, what on Mother's earth happened? Chris, answer me." She ran her hands gently over his body looking for other injuries but found none. His face was badly bruised and disfigured. His nose was crushed almost flat and blood covered him everywhere but no other injuries that she could see.

Rebecca fell to the floor behind him and cradled his head in her lap, slowly rubbing his temple and stroked his forehead. She knew him well, he had been a tag along with Clint and his much older friends. "Chris, wake up." She leaned over him whispering softly in his ear, continuing her caresses. "Come on Chris, open your eyes."

Chris gasped and slowly did as she said, looking around wildly. He calmed down when he finally focused on the two women bent over him. "Regina, Becca. How'd I get here?"

"That's what we would like to know but it'll wait until later." Regina whispered softly, as she tossed a light blanket to Becca so she could cover his nude body. "Just keep still for us until help comes, okay?" Leaving him and Rebecca, she called the paramedics then Chris's brother.

Regina quietly informed Rick Running Waters of the situations and made a rude noise when he gave one of his bellows over the phone. Holding the phone from her ear, she raised an eyebrow as a string of profanity flew through the line. She politely waited until he was finished then calmly told him to stop talking and to start driving before she hung up on him.

Rebecca held Chris's head gently whispering softly as her hands checked his face and head for further injuries. When she got to his nose and cheeks, he growled and tried to jerk away from the pain her light touch caused. "Easy Chris, I won't hurt you, I'm just checking."

He gasped and growled at the same time forcing him self to relax. "Sorry. I feel like I can't breath right." Swallowing he shuddered before coughing.

"I know, just breath through your mouth. Blood is draining into your sinuses." Looking up to her mother worried she shook her head slowly. The broken nose was just the tip of the injuries. His sinus cavity had to be damaged by the way he was struggling for breath. She took the towel from her mother's hand and gently wiped the blood from his gaping mouth. She knew that his injuries were serious and they could be fatal to some. She threw a questioning glance at the door and back at her mother. "How much longer?"

"Not much, just keep him calm." Kneeling Regina looked him in the eye as she wiped the blood from his mouth. "Who did this to you, Chris?"

"Don't know. On border watch east. Something hit me across nose. I remember falling out of the tree and that was it until I came to and ran. Saw the house and came here." Getting agitated he lifted his head growling.

"Easy big cat." Rebecca smiled and rubbed his forehead gently. "Don't get your blood pressure up. You'll be fine in a few minutes."

They heard the sirens approach the house and a car screech to a stop in the driveway ahead of the sirens. Rick's roar made Chris jump and he groaned weakly.

"What the hell happened, kid?" Rick ran up the steps, fell to his knees beside his little brother, and laid a tender hand on his shoulder.

"Attacked. Never saw 'em." Coughing he gasped as more blood flowed from his nose. "It hurts Rick." His brother's name came out slurred as he slipped into unconsciousness as Rebecca placed a firm finger on the soft spot at his temple.

She looked at Rick and shook her head slowly. "He's badly hurt and the more he struggles the more pain he's in. Let the paramedics get him to the clinic so they can fix him up before you start questioning him." She slowly slid from under Chris's head careful not to jar him too much. His blond hair sticking to her jeans where the blood had started to dry.

The men quickly helped her to stand and then took charge of their patient. Placing a c-collar on him, they then rolled him on to the stretcher keeping him on his side so he wouldn't choke on his blood.

Holding Rick's arm she kept him from following so she could have a private word with him. "We need to talk."

Rick looked down at her suddenly feeling a power coming from her hand, a strong unusual power. "I need to be with my brother." He tried to pull away but her grip held him in place.

"He's being taken care of and we need to tell you what he told us." Patting his arm, she pulled back. "He may not remember what he told us later."

"Okay, shoot." He watched the ambulance leave and tried to focus on what she was telling him. When she finished she had his full attention.

"This is the third attack of one of our border guardians in the last month." Taking a seat and accepting a cup of coffee from Regina, he closed his eyes and ducked his head, remembering she was an Elder of the Council. "I haven't said anything because I thought it wasn't serious. The others were jumped, tossed around some but no one was ever seriously injured until today."

Regina shook her head in disbelief. "You should have brought this to us and the Tribunal immediately Rick, you know that. Something this important shouldn't be kept a secret. It could turn out to be dangerous for everyone living here." Standing before him, her hands on hips, she scowled down at him. "I'm calling an emergency council meeting tonight for those on a need to know basis."

Seeing her mother look at her with "the look", she knew that she would be expected to sit in on the meeting. She also knew she was expected to keep quiet about it unless approached by a Guardian or a council member. This was not something that needed to become public knowledge, yet.

Rick stood and nodded to Regina with respect before shaking her hand. "I'll be in touch." Turning to Rebecca, he hesitated only a moment before clearing his throat. "Rebecca, I, ah,"

"Don't Rick." Holding up her hand, she shook her head. "I did what needed to be done to keep him calm. He will be okay but a little wary of me for a while. And when he realizes what I did, he's going to be mad as hell." Smiling smugly, she stood. "Our secret, Okay? I don't do it often but it had to be done today."

His surprised expression made her smile bigger showing off her deep dimples. "He was fighting his body's natural instinct to pass out and I just gave him a little push." Shrugging she walked him to the door. "Go see your brother Rick. He is going to need you when he wakes up."

Opening the door, he nodded dumbfounded. "Hey, Rebecca thanks." He paused, about to tell her about Cole's visit but thought better of it. The Red Feather women did not need to know about that yet, if ever.

Sitting through the opening minutes of the council's meeting Rebecca let her mind wander settling on the point of how she came to be sitting in front of them tonight.

She had loved growing up here but always felt she had a mission in life and that was to leave. When she finally left, she had her purpose and it was research, Native American History to be precise. She got her doctorate early having been able to skip grades in her education. Staying focused had helped her to achieve her goal of a doctorate degree and when she achieved it, she began her real passion. Finding anything and everything, she could about her people through the other Native American Nations.

So far, she had found only what others deemed ancient folklore, legends or myths, bits and pieces scattered through out the country. Which was good news for everyone concerned, their abilities could prove to be their demise if found out by the wrong people. She made monthly reports to the group of elected Elders known as the Council of her findings and so far, they weren't worried. But since her last report things had changed and she had something important to report.

Standing before the entire Council that night she calmly gave her version of the day's events. She admitted that she had knocked Chris out to keep him calm for his own good.

The council didn't seem surprised by her admission; they actually accepted it as a natural occurrence of power. She spent a few minutes nervously answering their questions on the extent of her abilities and she had to confess she had been having dreams of warning. She told them about the eyes, the black form, and the feelings she got during the dreams. Telling them she had been warned by Clint's spirit that evil was here, caused a stir.

Max finally stood and pounded his fist on the table for silence. "We're here to discuss the attacks and any other pertinent information folks. And we can't do that with everyone shouting." Giving everyone a stern look and winking at his granddaughter, he took his seat again. "Three attacks in as many weeks are troublesome especially when they only happen on only the eastern border." Pausing he bowed his head as if in deep thought before speaking again. "We have a problem and we need to get a handle on it before it gets out of control, fast. I fear it's going to lead to strangers coming here, leading us to disaster." Rubbing his temples, he sighed. "Any ideas?"

The council members talked quietly amongst themselves for a long time but no one could offer a good plan. Rebecca fidgeted in her chair feeling as if she was being watched closely during the discussions. Closing her eyes, she thought back to the day she arrived home and those hair-raising moments on the edge of that cliff.

Jumping to her feet she quietly cleared her throat until she got her grandfather's attention. "May I please address the council again?"

Everyone stopped talking and looked at her as if they just realized she was still there. Max did not get any objections so he waved her to come forward and speak.

"I'm not sure if this has anything to do with this situation."

"Tell us anyway child. We're stymied and just talking in circles."

"Who was the guard assigned to the southern road a few days ago?" Keeping her voice calm she hoped she looked as calm. "I almost slid off that hairpin turn because someone was sitting in the middle of it. Scared the tar out of me when he just appeared like that out of the trees."

Everyone looked at Rick since he was the one in charge of the border guardians and handed out assignments to them. Clearing his throat, he raised a finger as he closed his eyes and meditated for a moment on who was assigned where. "I believe Miles Darkwing had that post until yesterday but he wasn't supposed to be at that spot, he was assigned to patrol the bottom of that grade." Opening his eyes, he cocked his head at Rebecca, frowning. "You're sure it was at that curve?"

"Positive. I always slow down for it because it's so tight and too close to the edge." Laughing nervously she placed her hands on the table. "I've scared my self silly on that curve too many times not to be cautious now."

"I'll ask him about it. This isn't the first time he's wandered away from his assigned post nor is this the first time he's pulled a stunt like that." Rick sat back as he wrote a quick note to bring the little jerk in for a chat. "I'll take care of it, I promise." Looking over his left shoulder, he jerked his head at someone.

Rebecca glanced to where he had nodded and saw someone step out of the shadows, barely containing her gasp. The familiar stance, hooded eyes and slightly lopsided grin was enough to make her heart skip a beat before it turned ice cold.

Cole.

She hadn't realize he had been there leaning against the wall during the entire meeting. He looked relaxed but his eyes were dark, showing no emotion except anger.

Swinging her eyes to her grandfather seeking an answer to her unspoken question of what's he doing here, she frowned. His quick head shake and blank face gave away nothing as she swallowed nervously. Turning to leave she stopped when she heard her grandfather clear his throat, looking over her shoulder she saw his slight head shake. She couldn't face him again, not now. She was too raw emotionally.

Sitting down she ducked her head wishing the floor would open up and swallow her up completely. Grinding her teeth she silently seethed as she pointedly kept her eyes on the other members to the right of the room when she finally raised her head. She wasn't about to let him know that his presence shook her deeply. It wasn't any of his business or right anymore.

As the council discussed their business, Cole had watched her through lowered lashes, keeping to the shadows. He had seen her arrive and couldn't deny she still held a large spot in his heart and soul. Hearing her greet everyone with her lilting voice had made him feel like he had been punched in the gut, astounding him. The room had gotten warm quickly from her smile, small laughs which were real this evening thought they were aimed at everyone but him.

Now that she saw him the room had grown chilly and bleak, her stiff posture said she was ignoring him and she was livid inside. He caught the slight flutter of her hand as she tucked a stray hair behind her tiny shell of an ear and he grinned to himself, scratching his jaw. She was nervous as hell and she knew he was watching her still.

He missed the question Max had asked him but caught Rick's quick movement. Reading Rick's lips, he caught the question and cleared his throat.   Straightening he stepped out to the end of the tables and shrugged a stiff shoulder. "We haven't heard anything unusual lately. Some of the teens have been seen sneaking out late at night." Grinning at the council, he glanced over at Becca remembering they did the same thing when they were younger. "They're mostly running the woods having fun, nothing to worry about."

Nodding to the council he laughed as they grinned remembering their own escapades. "I've seen mostly wolves, but an occasional bear and some prey birds. Nothing surprising as spring is in full swing and the weather has been pretty good this year."

Max chuckled and sat back in his seat watching the two young people. "I would be worried if the young didn't let loose." He remembered harsher springs making the times harder, then all hell would break loose because the young had been pent up too long.

"I hate to change the subject but we've noticed more drug related busts."

Grimacing he brought up the one big concern the Guardians had lately. "It's more then just a few ounces of pot lately. We've been finding Crack Cocaine, Meth, Speed and Ecstasy in Indian Mound and unfortunately it's a lot for this size of an area." He held his hand up when the members started asking questions loudly over each other. "We don't know when or where they're coming from nor do we know who is selling the crap. Yet. And yes when we do know whose dealing we'll take care of it."

Rick stood and held his hand up for quiet again. "Folks, please. We have noticed the trend and we are dealing with it as best as we can. When we get some good reliable information, we will move in. I've already asked the Tribunal for more funds so I can hire a few more Guardians and get some newer up to date equipment." He rolled his eyes at his deputy when someone demanded a specific time frame as to when they would put a stop to the drug problem.

Cole shook his head and clamped a hand on Rick's shoulder. "We can't give you all a set time frame. Can you give us a set time as to when you're going to sneeze next?"

Several chuckles silenced the rest of the questions as they realized they were asking for a miracle fix. "We'll take care of it when the time comes, never fear." Nodding to Max he glanced at Rebecca and gave her a slow wink before he went back to lean against his wall.

"Okay folks, we've got one more piece of business we should get cleared up and then we'll call it a night." Max stood again and held his hand up to silence the many groans. "We've all had time to mull over the offer made by that lumber company."

Rebecca listened with half an ear as she snuck a sideways glance at Cole, clinching her teeth at his wink. She could not believe he had been so arrogant and still be so good looking at the same time. Clamping down on that stray thought, she turned her head to stare at the opposite wall.

She heard her grandfather explain the company's offer of harvesting over several thousand acres of trees, replacing them as they went north and east of the valley. She also heard several members grumble at the extent of the proposed harvest.

When Pete stood to be recognized, Max sat giving him the floor. Pete held a thick binder in his hand and quickly explained his research and findings. Shaking his head, he tapped the binder on the table. "I've been asking around and I always get the same response. They are the shadiest company around. They have repeatedly lied, broken or not completed contracts with other places. So, please, read my report and decide later." He stood taller and cleared his throat again. "I think even considering this offer is wrong, I feel it in my bones."

Max nodded and rested his arms on the table. "Okay everyone, get a copy, read it and we'll vote after Equinox." Seeing everyone in agreement, he checked his watch. "Anything else?"

"Yeah." Allen Bearstone jumped up before anyone could object. "I want to file a complaint against Darkwing. He's out of control and he's pushing his luck."

He shot a scowl at Rick before continuing. "Either the Guardians take care of him or I will. Permanently. Martha had another run in with him today. This time he walked right into our house and she had to throw him out physically. I'm not letting him get another chance to pull another stunt like this."

Rick jumped up and gave a bellow over the voices of the others as Cole strode to Allen's side grabbing his arm. Rick's bellow bounced off the wooden walls silencing everyone. "Allen, you need to keep your cool and your spirit under control. We will handle Darkwing, you hear me? We. Will. Handle. Him."

She watched Cole slowly release his tight grip on Allen's arm knowing he could take Allen to the floor quickly if need be. She felt his eyes on her and met his stare but only for a moment before lowering her eyelids.

He was trying to reach her like when they were younger but she rejected him. She couldn't let him see she still held a small piece of him buried deep inside and she couldn't allow herself to fall under that magic again.

Cole whispered something in Allen's ear bringing a smug look to the man's face and slowly stepped back when Allen nodded relaxing. She watched Cole through her eyelashes as he walked back to stand beside his boss frowning and quickly turned her head when he glanced back at her.

"Right now our hands are tied where Darkwing is concerned. No one has filed an official criminal complaint so legally our hands are tied." Running his fingers through his already mussed hair Rick sighed. "I'm afraid someone is going to get hurt or seriously threatened before we can do anything about him."

"I heard Martha chased him off and he left a trail behind him to the front door." Rebecca piped up trying to ease the tension in the room. Seeing Allen's beam of pride she felt the tension drop by half.

"She's awful proud of herself lately." Shrugging he grinned from ear to ear before nodding to Max. "My apologies Elder, ladies and gentlemen. I just cannot abide a man harassing our women folk. I let my temper get the best of me." He sat down and bowed his head.

Max accepted the apology and looked around the table for any other speakers, seeing none he quickly called a close to the meeting by rapping on the table twice with his walking stick.

As everyone filed out Rebecca hung back to wait for a chance to ask Rick how his brother was doing. Her timing was off and she found herself face to face with the one person she had no desire to speak with

Before she could make her escape, he moved quickly to her side and grabbed her arm pulling her close. He looked down at her wide eyes and he felt himself fall into the pools of liquid brown. His first instinct was to kiss her quivering lips hard until she melted against him and the second was to shake her senseless but he held himself in check.

"Becca, we need to talk." Growling he refused to release his grip on her jerking arm. "But not here. Can we go some where more private?"

She could feel the flames of anger grow inside and her skin heated in response. "It'll be a cold day in hell when we talk again Cole. I have nothing to say and I am sure you have nothing I want or need to hear. You said enough the day you tucked tail and ran." Hissing at him, she began yanking her arm to get free knowing she would have bruises by morning. When he wouldn't let her go, she showed her teeth, smiling sweetly. "Let me go Cole, right now or you won't like my reaction."

Bringing her against him, he pulled her arm behind her back trapping her. Catching her delicate chin with his free hand, he tipped her head slightly. It would have been so easy to capture her mouth, teeth included but he hesitated. "We will talk Rebecca, you can count on it." Growling he lowered his head and inched closer. "You can count on it." Just before he got his first taste of her in four long lonely years, she snapped at him. He felt her bite on his bottom lip and the blood as it spurted against his tongue.

She quickly stepped away when his grip loosened, putting some distance between them. Wiping the back of her hand across her burning lips, she watched as he dabbed a finger at his bleeding lip. "Next time I'll give you more then a bloody lip Cole. I mean it, stay away from me."

He watched her back away, feeling as if he had gotten a punch in the throat, his lip burned and it only added fuel to the fire inside. "You drew first blood Becca, like or not I will win and we will talk."

She stepped further back holding out her hands in warning. "You drew first blood four years ago Cole, not me. You left me here with a broken and bleeding heart. As far as I am concerned, we are finally even. Just stay away." Spinning she dashed to the open door and out into the dark night.

He clinched his fists gulping in air to his burning lungs as he stared after her. He wished to hell now that he had not approached her or lost control having her body pressed against him like that. But the need to touch her, to hold her, to taste her sweet mouth had been too much for him and his spirits.

This was the second time today she had ran from him and this time he was not going to let her get away with it. His animalistic side had taken over before he could put a stop to it. Hell, they were still clamoring for him to go after her. When the night swallowed her completely he gave out a loud howl of frustration, want and need.

Spinning he stalked to the door ready to chase her down, ignoring his head when it screamed at him for him to back off. Scanning the area, he saw nothing but he quickly caught her scent not far ahead of him in the darkness. She smelt of woman, earth and anger, sending excitement through him as no other woman ever had.

He couldn't fight the demands of his spirits any longer and took off after her, their determination drove him. He had to push her, make her listen and he had to win. Now was the time for all or nothing.

He had almost caught up to her and her intoxicating scent but skidded to a stop when he saw her standing in the middle of some vacant lots. She just stood there, arms wrapped around her stomach shaking violently and sobbing hysterically.

He felt confusion from his spirits as she angrily wiped away her tears, muttering to herself. He began to wonder if there was something besides him eating at her. Stepped from behind the gigantic oak, snapping a twig under his foot, he inevitably announced his presence. "Do you really hate me that much?"

She spun in surprise, her loose hair flying around her like a dark cloud. "I told you to stay away." Screeching at him, she clinched her fists at her sides. "Can't you get it through your thick skull? I don't want to talk to you or even smell you." She turned her back to him knowing it could be a costly mistake. Looking over her shoulder, she whispered softly. "Leave me alone Cole."

"I can't." He sighed as he silently stepped closer until he was so close she could feel his breath through her hair. "They won't let me." He reached for her arm but pulled back when he saw the red marks on her arm. "I'm sorry."

She felt him move closer behind her and stepped away, putting a little distance between them. "Why? Because you manhandled me when you grabbed my arm? Because you left us to grieve and bury my brother, alone?" Turning to face him, she waved her hands wildly as she continued to screech at him. "Because you weren't there when he died, alone? Or because you were a coward and ran away?"

Her screeching accusations made him flinch and she felt little satisfaction in her cruel words. "You could apologize for the rest of your natural days Cole but it won't mean a tinker's damn to me." Shaking her head, she tried to make the sudden loud ringing in her head go away.

Cole watched her as her body began to shake violently, her dark eyes began to glow angrily, and her hair seemed to fan out around her as she swung around as if she was being caught between two forces. It was frightening to see her like this and at the same time he felt drawn to it. He had not realized he had stepped closer to her until he felt her hair lash at his face.

He could feel her rage, fear and emptiness coming from her as she began keening as if she was grieving. He felt the high-pitched keening in his head and clasped his hands over his ears to block out the sounds. Falling to his knees he watched as the white of her eyes began to brighten as her pupils dilated.

Struggling to his feet, he reached out to her only to have his hands thrust away violently as she spun towards the left then right again as if fighting to grab hold of something he couldn't see. Crying out her name, he tried again and finally caught her by her shoulders, struggling to hold on to her tightly.

She only saw her spirits standing on either side of her, their backs facing her and moving as if to leave. She tried to reach out to them but something stopped her, screaming she caught them but they struggled, fighting against her. Begging, she felt them relent but they still wouldn't face her. She didn't see Cole as he reached for her until he finally caught her. She only realized her head was held still while her body shook wildly.

"Becca, stop it. Becca, knock it off!" He kept his voice steady but forceful as he clasped her face between his gentle hands.

She broke the spell she had been under by shaking her head quickly, blinking until her eyes focused on him. "Get your hands off of me!" She jerked to get away from him but his hands tightened holding her in place, burning her with his touch.

"Not until you get yourself under control!" He gasped as if he was trying to catch his breath as if he had been running for miles. "Get a grip on yourself."

Taking a shaky breath, she tried to push his arms away but his tight muscles would not give. Dropping her hands to her sides, she gave up fighting, heaving a sigh and hung her head. "Please, let me go Cole."

He loosened his grip enough to drop his hands and gently knead her tense shoulders, trying to help her calm down. "I will when I'm sure you won't go off like that again."

Jerking her head up, she frowned. "Off like what? What are you talking about?" She noticed the fine welts rising on his cheeks and his heaving chest. "What happened to you?"

"You happened, don't you remember?' He looked at her with troubled eyes and confusion written all over his face. "You were fighting with something that wasn't there."

Starting to deny it, she clamped her lips closed as a vision of her hair flying around her and a bone chilling cold filling her. She remembered wind whipping at her, trying to tear her apart from her spirits. "I did that?"

Her eyes went wide with understanding and fear. "I couldn't stop it. It just exploded out of me." As the fear grew she began shaking uncontrollably, her teeth chattering as the ice cold settled deep inside her.

"Calm down Becca." He gently pulled her head up and searched her face for signs of anger. "Just relax and think about what brought this on." Rubbing his thumb across her damp cheek, he took a deep breath and groaned softly.

She could see him struggling with something until he got himself under control with a shiver of his own. "I don't know. I left you at the Council building and started running towards home. I felt anger, strong anger and then intense pain inside." She blinked slowly as another emotion welled up in her, deep loneliness. "I felt alone as if a part of me left. The emptiness happened so fast it felt like my soul was being ripped out of me." Her hot tears spilled over, running down her face splashing on his hands as she turned her head. "I couldn't stop it." Gasping she covered her face. "I couldn't stop it."

Cole pulled her into his arms and gently rocked her as the gut wrenching sobs came again. "It's okay Becca, let it out. Let it go." Rubbing her back, he simply held her as her tears fell, silently encouraging her to let it out.

Rebecca felt as if a overstressed dam wall had finally gave, everything flooded out at once when she didn't have the strength to hold it in anymore or the strength to fight the churning waters. When Cole wrapped his arms around her tighter, her emotional state worsened. She felt like she was being drained of all her anger, grief and pain only to have it all replaced by loneliness and emptiness.

When her sobs began to weaken, she found she couldn't breathe and began struggling in his arms. She tried to pull away but he would not let her go. Gasping she started to panic, feeling her lungs begin to burn. "Cole, let me go," she began to struggle harder desperate for air. "I can't breathe."

Feeling him loosen his hold, she gulped in air, leaning her forehead against his rib cage just below his pounding heart. She didn't realize she had begun to match her breathing to his steady rhythm until the dancing stars behind her eyes faded. "I don't know why I'm doing this. I'm sorry for being such a baby." Mumbling she wiped the tears from her eyes. "I never reacted like this before."

Cole stepped back gently holding her arms and bent to look into her hidden face. "Look at me Becca." Tipping her head up by her chin, he searched her tear streaked face. Giving her a weak smile, he tucked her hair behind her ear.

She saw compassion, tenderness and strain in his eyes and when she looked closer, she actually saw what looked like tears. "Shhh, don't cry Cole."

He gave a raspy laugh as he laid his hand to her cheek. "I should have told you that Becca, not the other way around."

She only then noticed he had changed a lot in four years. There were fine lines around his sad eyes and he looked much older then his thirty-three years. Looking at his mouth, she saw the cut she had inflicted on him earlier and cringed. "I'm sorry," she whispered slowly reaching up a finger to it. "Does it hurt?"

"Not too bad." Dropping his hands, he slowly moved away, giving them space and her a lopsided grin. "I've gotten worse tussling with a bunch of bears."

She rubbed her arms as the air turned chilly around her trying not to let him see her small grin. Looking up at him once she got her lips to behave, she couldn't find any of the bitter anger or pain she had cultivated towards him over the last few years anymore. "Why did you leave Cole?" Asking gently she did not want an intense argument to break out again. She wanted understanding now, no fighting, no accusations and no hiding anymore.

"I tried to explain it to you in the letter, Becca." Shoving his hands in his back pockets, he braced himself as if he expected another yelling match to start. "I explained everything in the letter."

"I only got letters three months after you left." She didn't add that those letters were still unopened. Rubbing her arms harder she waited for his answer. Seeing him close in on himself, she pushed. "Why Cole? My family needed you and I needed you then." She reached for him but could not touch him much as she wanted to feel his warmth.

"I couldn't take the accusations from everyone, including from my own father. However, the worse was the accusation I saw in your eyes. It almost killed me to think that you of all people blamed me, so I left."

Watching him closely she knew in her heart he was telling her the painful truth. The pain he still felt was there, written all over his face and in his body language. "But when the final report came back, why didn't you return?" Throwing her out her hand, she swept the air. "You had no reason to stay away anymore, Cole."

"I thought I did. You hated me and someone let it slip that you found someone to replace me shortly afterwards." His eyes never left her, hiding nothing, not his pain, his regret or his shame.

She was stunned and held up a hand to stop him from going on. "I never turned to another man, I held out for you to return. And when you didn't come back after a few months, I left." Placing a hand over her heart, she took a shaky breath. "I was in love with you Cole and I thought you felt the same towards me."

"Oh Becca, I loved you with all my heart but when I heard that you found someone else, knowing you were in the arms of another man, I kept away. I couldn't face you, seeing you with someone else. The only reason I came back was because my father was dying." Looking to the night sky he stopped speaking and worked his jaw as if he was about to admit something.

"That doesn't explain why you left before Clint's service. Why then?" She couldn't stop the prodding questions from pouring out. It was almost as if she was begging for new pain to replace the old. "Why?"

He stood there shaking his head sadly. "You asked me the same thing back then. " 'Why? Why wasn't I there with him that day?' Do you remember?"

"I don't." She whispered hoarsely bowing her head. "I don't remember much after they told me that he was dead and I saw you being dragged away by the Guardians." New anger welled up but this time aimed at her self. She hadn't even tried to find out why he had been taken into custody. "What really happened that day?"

Chapter 3

"I got a call from the Tribunal that morning, to report to them for some questions they had about a stupid fight I got into. I had just joined the Guardians then and they raked me over the coals good. I should have known better, they said. They finally dismissed me after two hours of questions and lectures. Right after that, I headed straight to the cliffs. By then it was too late."

She opened her mouth but nothing came out as his words sank in. She could see his emotional scars so close to the surface and in his eyes. "You couldn't have done anything, could you?"

"No. I couldn't even tell him I was sorry." Looking at his feet, he took a ragged breath. "I should have been there, for both of you."

Stepping up to him, she placed a gentle hand over his heart. "It's never too late to say you're sorry and I think he knew."

Cole captured her slender fingers against his chest and slowly caressed them with a calloused thumb. "What about you Becca? Is it too late to say I'm sorry and maybe have a chance to start over?"

Her breath caught in her throat as his eyes burned with hope and longing. "I don't know if I'm ready for that Cole. Not yet." She watched as the hope in his eyes fade and he closed into himself. She couldn't help herself when she gasped as he pulled her hand away and stepped back. "Cole, please understand what I'm trying to say."

"I understand better then you think, Rebecca." Whispering sadly, he shook his head. "You've been through enough lately and I'm afraid I'm only making it worse." Turning he shoved his hands into his pockets. "Go home Becca. Please, go home." Growling over his shoulder at her, he closed his eyes as if he couldn't stand to see any more of her pain. "Just promise me that you'll think about what I've said and when you're ready, you know how to find me."

Watching him walk away, she wiped a new tear from her face as his stiff back disappeared into the night, making her bow her head in regret. Telling herself he was right in telling her to go home, she slowly began walking in the opposite direction feeling as if she was making the wrong choice.

As she got closer to home, she sensed she was being followed, Casting her eyes to the sidewalk and the dark shadows beyond them, the hair on her arms raised in alarm, someone was pacing her off of her right side. She caught the scent of wolf, a hunting, hungry wolf. Rubbing her arms she debated if she should make a run for the house or stay calm, facing it. There was no telling who was out there and for all she knew it could be one of the many teenagers having themselves a little game at her expense.

Keeping to the middle of the lit street, in plain view, she caught a flash of mangy brown fur around glowing black eyes and she stumbled. Those eyes stared at her menacing intent and its teeth were bared in a snarl, sending shivers up her spine. They almost looked like the ones in her dream but they were too unfocused.

She knew she was in trouble when it stopped, facing her and slowly crouched, readying to jump at her. She could not think fast enough to change herself and when she finally tried, nothing happened. Just then a much bigger wolf jumped between her and her aggressor she gave a small cry as she stumbling back a step. The new wolf had its hackles raised and showed it bared teeth angrily as it paced in front of her.

She watched as the two faced off, trying to stare each other down and growled deep warnings. She knew she should run but instinct told her that doing so would be very dangerous right now and changing, if she could, would be just as dangerous if not fatal. Standing as if frozen she did not interfere or call attention to herself, letting them settle the matter between them.

The black wolf never lowered his head giving a low rumbling growl, telling the smaller wolf to leave his chosen alone. He did not know this wolf but that didn't stop him from stepping closer, pushing his alpha status. He knew Becca could have fallen victim to this wolf and he could not allow it in any way. No one had the right to approach her or dare to touch her, no one other then him.

The brown wolf slowly lowered his head in submission as it back stepped still baring its fangs. It stopped growling, having not counting on the interference of a more dominate wolf. He knew he was out weighed and out muscled by the black wolf. Cutting his loses he quickly turned and took off in the opposite direction in a dead run, his tail tucked between his legs.

Cole gave chase, following until he lost the others scent halfway across the commons. Zigzagging he tried to pick up the trail but couldn't find any hint of where he was hiding. After a few minutes of searching, he finally gave up, snarled in frustration and ran back to where they had left Rebecca standing.

She was gone though he caught her scent easily enough and knew she had wisely decided to hightail it home as soon as they had ran off. Walking slowly down the middle of the street, he followed her, letting her enter the house undisturbed.

He could see her standing in the house, peering out the front window and he knew she could see him clearly still walking up the street slowly. When he stopped at the edge of the driveway, he saw her put her hand to her throat and he nodded once to her as if to say it was done.

They stared at each other through the window for a minute until he couldn't take it anymore. Turning, he headed north, slipping into the shadows before looking back over his shoulder. He thought he heard a door open but couldn't be sure. He did hear a soft 'thank you' float on the air and he was glad to know he had stopped a catastrophe by letting his animalistic side take over to follow her home.

Rebecca didn't recognize or rightly care who had jumped to her aid but she was safe because of him. Saying thank you didn't repay the rescuer but it was all she had to offer for now. Standing just outside the door she searched for the wolf but couldn't see him.

As she locked the door behind her, she shuddered. Someone had meant her harm tonight and it shook her. She also felt anger towards herself. She didn't defend herself, hadn't even shift changed. She knew she was out of practice but to be that frightened was inexcusable. She thought her instincts were shaper then that.

Pacing before the fireplace, she hugged herself tightly. She should have been able to detect danger long before she actually did, but her mind had been too focused on Cole.

Of course, seeing Cole had unhinged her at first and then his approaching her hadn't helped. Remembering the look on his face and his turned back, she sniffed and wiped away a stray tear. "I don't understand my life anymore", she whispered to the dying fire. "Why did it get so complicated?"

"Because you can't let go and he still cares." Her grandfather whispered from the kitchen door, leaning against the doorframe, taking a bite of pie.

Chewing, he ignored her scowl while he waved his fork around. "A man with his spirits dares to care a lot. You should know that better then anyone."

She turned her back to the fire ignoring the popping embers. "You knew he was going to approach me and you didn't even warn me. How come?"

"Not my place," he mumbled around another mouthful. "You're grown and it's time you started taking care of your own life." Walking to the easy chair he folded himself into it and propped his bare feet on the coffee table. "I think you've been unreasonable and stupid for treating Cole like you have been."

"Unreasonable, stupid? That's harsh Grandda and very untrue." She turned to glare at the fire again. She knew he could be cruel when he wanted to be but not that cruel especially when she was already feeling raw inside and out.

"Yeah and blind on top of it." He enjoyed pushing her buttons right now because he could see her real feelings beginning to come out finally. He knew in his heart she needed to get some of that pent up anger and bitterness out before it poisoned her soul. "You refuse to see that Cole still cares and wants to make amends. However, you won't let him. Instead you just throw up bigger, thicker walls. One of these days he's going to give up and you'll be nothing but a prisoner of your own making."

He stared at her stiff back and sighed. "You are a fool if you don't give him a chance. Besides, I don't think Clint would approve of your stubborn pride turning you into a bitter old woman."

Rebecca spun and stomped across the room to stand beside her grandfather. "Bitter old woman?' she practically screeched at him waving her hands wildly. "I'm not like that!"

"Yes you are!" he calmly replied placing his empty plate on the side table. "You are and it's eating you up inside. You don't even realize it's affecting your spirits, do you?" He calmly reached for her hand hanging limply at her side. "When was the last time you've flown or ran free other then in your dreams child?" He could see it in her eyes, the struggle between telling the truth and the need to lie. Standing in front of her, he wrapped his arms around her small shoulders. "I know child but if you don't stop this you'll die inside and more then just your heart and soul will be lost."

She listened with her heart and knew he was right. She had known for some time her spirits were slowly fading away but had foolishly blocked it from her mind. Hence the struggle Cole had witnessed and her inability to change swiftly when confronted by the brown wolf. She was lucky if she could to do small partial changes and that ability had become extremely difficult as of late. "I don't know what to do Grandda." She sobbed as she realized her vision warned her that her spirits were so close to leaving her. "I'm scared."

"Don't be, it's not too late." He rocked her gently and softly began to hum an old chant. When she stopped struggling in his arms, he began singing the words softly to her in the quiet room.

As she felt his words float around and caress her, she slowly relaxed. As weariness washed over her, she felt herself slipping into a peaceful oblivion before she could say that she and Cole had talked.

Max gently held her as the chant worked its magic and as her knees buckled, he gathered her into his arms as he did when she was little. Carrying her limp body up to her room, he continued to chant softly laying his cheek against her head. Passing a stunned Regina in the hall, he nodded and smiled sadly. She followed and lent her soft voice to his deeper one as she held her daughters limp hand.

As Max laid Rebecca on her bed, he raised his hands up to the sky and closed his eyes. He called to her spirits asking them to return and lend their strength to her for what was to come. Looking down on her he saw her facial features quickly change and knew they would stay with her, for now.

Cole had snuck around to the back of Rebecca's house and sat watching her through the back window, from the shadows. He witnessed her argument with Max, amazed at the older man's calm demeanor while she waved her hands wildly. He was also amazed when Max calmly held her and she slowly melted in his arms. Cole heard or rather felt the chant in his head and had to shake himself to keep from letting it take hold over him. He saw Rebecca's soft bedroom light go on and heard another softer voice join the chant.

He watched as a shadow raise its hands and heard the ancient words calling for strength and unity. He was surprised he understood them but being in wolf form allowed it. He felt his eagle's keen interest in the words and felt it become less agitated as the voice spoke.

He saw Max step to the window and he crept further into the shadows but Max looked down and directly in to his eyes. He barely caught the Shamans whisper on the wind, "She'll rest now. Give her time young one, four years worth of healing does not happen over night. Go home." Max quietly closed the window and turned off the light.

Cole sat silently watching, listening for another hour but the house went dark and all was quiet. He felt confused by all that had transpired tonight and he needed time to think.

Taking off in a smooth lope, he made his way home, stopping every so often to sniff the air. When he passed the council building, he remembered that he had left the lights burning when he had taken off to chase Becca. Circling to go back, he found it dark and locked up, safe and secure. Sniffing the door, the steps and surrounding area, he caught the scent of Running Water and relaxed, knowing that Rick had taken care of it on his last round of the night.

Racing home, he let out a howl and paused when it echoed through the valley back to him. It still sounded lonely and forlorn but the last echo carried a note of hope in it. He lifted his head when he heard a faint reply and wondered if she had instinctively answered or if someone else finally understood how he felt.

Once he reached the lane, he changed back to his human form and walked up to the house in his bare skin. The damp air held the promise of more moisture but cooled his heated skin. Shaking his head, he still could not believe what he had seen and been through during the day. So much had been cleared up but a lot of it left him with only more questions, confusing him.

He was relieved when his gut told him to follow her home and his wolf had followed that feeling because if he hadn't who knows what could have happened. He just wished that he could have caught the mutt who threatened Becca and given him a fight he would never forget, if he survived that is.

Opening the door, he caught the sound of thunder far out in the west, far enough off that it wouldn't reach them until late tomorrow or the next day, if it came at all. Looking up he saw some clouds rolling in covering the almost full moon at times. He loved storms and his senses told him that this one would come and it would be one of the strong ones.

Without turning on the lights he climbed the stairs and headed for the master bathroom and a shower. Standing under the hot pulsating spray he heard the thunder rolling again and hung his head. He felt like that thunder, making a lot of noise, shaking everything around but no real threat to anyone.

Thinking of the last few hours, he sagged against the tiled wall remembering following Becca home. She had made it safe and unharmed though he knew she was upset. It was evident by her jerky pacing inside and she had every right to be. What really bothered him was that she hadn't done anything to protect herself. She had just stood there when she was threatened.

She was as capable as anyone here is to shift but she hadn't and that in itself was odd as hell. Then having Max calling to spirits, asking them to return and strengthen was also weird in his book.

Feeling the water getting cold, he turned the shower off and grabbed a large towel. Drying himself, he thought he heard soft chanting way off in the distance slowly wrapping itself around him like a blanket, soft and comfortable.

Laying across the king sized bed he laid an arm across his eyes and felt the chant get a little stronger until he drifted off to sleep, barely catching the whispered, 'and rest now,' echo gently in his head.

The next morning Rebecca practically jumped out of bed feeling as if she could take on the whole world. She dressed quickly and realized she hadn't slept that peaceful in years. She did remember her dreams and the painfully lonely call that stirred them. She had answered that call with one of her own and when she went in search of that lonely call, she looked everywhere. She tried to find him but never found the caller though she raced to follow it through the dense forest.

As she stared at her reflection, she noticed that the dark circles under her eyes seem to have faded a little over night and her face had lost some of its tight pinched look too. Shaking her head, she couldn't decide whether to be angry with her grandfather or just thank him for stepping in.

When she finally went down, she caught her family's laughter coming from the back deck through the open door. Catching her mother's wave she smiled and motioned her that she would join them in a minute. Her grandfather grinned smugly over his shoulder as he waved his cup asking for more coffee.

Getting her cup, she grabbed the insulated pot and took it out with her. Kissing her mothers cheek as she filled her cup, she gave a small laugh when she was rewarded with a loving pat on the cheek. Stepping to her grandfather's side, she looked down at him and held the pot out of his long reach. "I should be mad at you, old sneak but thanks." Grinning she winked and then filled his cup smirking. "You know I'll have to get even some day."

"Likely story kiddo." Waving her thanks away, he stared across the property. "I couldn't let you keep on that path anymore, child. It was slowly poisoning you and I will not allow you to do that to yourself." He squinted up to her sighing. "You're too important to our people and us."

She caught her breath at the sincerity in his voice and the haunted look on his face. It shook her to realize she hadn't seen what she was doing and how bad it was affecting her or her family. To have her grandfather take matters into his loving hands without offering first was saying a lot.

"Well I'm glad you stepped in Grandda though I have to admit it could have happened sooner." She sat beside her mother and peered into her cup. Slowly she told them about her stalker and now admitted aloud her inability to change, moreover to protect her self. She didn't give either of them a chance to interrupt as she continued, when she finally finished she ducked her head in shame. "I let the fear take control and it scares me."

"Well it's all behind you child. But do you have any idea who the brown wolf was?"

Looking up, she shook her head and felt her mothers hand still her nervously bouncing knee. "No idea. I caught his stink just before he stepped out of the shadows. I have never seen him before. Oh wait." She sat straighter almost tipping her coffee on to the table. "Miles. Miles was the wolf. I just remembered him from the first day home. But why would he be hunting me?"

Looking at her grandfather, she saw dark clouds gathering in his narrow eyes. "Grandda, we've got to find that black wolf. We have to report this to Rick."

"We will but I don't think you're going to be happy about who your rescuer was." He wiped a weathered hand down his face slowly. "I know who the black wolf is and he's probably in Rick's office right now making his own report. I would say that we could expect company before too long. But before they get here we need to get something aired." He leaned across the table and laid a hand on her stiff arm.

"You've got a long, rough road ahead of you and I need you to keep your head." He tilted his head until he looked into her troubled eyes. "Your spirits are strong, and they will not leave you. However, you need to let them loose. Before the day is over you need to let one of them go free. They're like caged animals locked inside you and they can become dangerous to you and everyone else." He squeezed her arm making sure she understood. "If you don't do this now you'll never become a whole person again. Do you understand what I'm trying to tell you?"

Nodding she took a shaky breath and knowing he was letting her imagine what could possibly happen. "I understand Grandda. I just didn't realize how close I was. You're right though. Dream casting isn't enough anymore is it?"

"For a small period of time it works fine but you've caged them inside for almost four years. That's too long and too dangerous."

"I know I've got a lot to make up for don't I?" Hiding her face in shame, she silently sent apologies to her spirits and asked for their forgiveness.

"More then you know but let's get your spirits healthy first before you go on to the next step. Okay?" Regina caressed her daughter's hair gently. "It'll be okay honey. We'll be here to help." Tipping her daughters face up, she caught a tear with her thumb. "We'll help where we can, I promise."

Rebecca took a deep shaky breath and nodded slowly. "If it's okay with you two I'll disappear after lunch and head north. I'll go to our meadow and run for a bit." Feeling better with her decision, she gave them a weak smile. "That's where most of my dreams take place anyway."

"Good choice." Max slapped the arms of his wooden chair satisfied with her decision. "Now, we should be getting visitors shortly. 'Gina, best put on more coffee and Becca, go dry your eyes." He chuckled when Regina bristled as her shortened name. "I'll keep them stalled until Rebecca's ready to face them. You need to clear your head, child. I figure you've got about five or so minutes."

The women rose and Rebecca paused beside Max on her way in to the house. "Thanks for everything Grandfather." Pressing a kiss on his fore head, she gave a small laugh. "You saved me, ya know."

"Naw just gave you a push back on to the right path." He patted her hand. "Just a very hard push is all." He ducked his head when she tried to ruffle his hair. "Go on, get yourself straightened up."

Hearing Rick's arrival, she took several deep, calming breaths and wiped her damp hands down her pants. Leaving her room, she listened to the voices as they floated up the stairs towards her. She recognized her grandfathers immediately and Rick's but the third voice was too low but sounded tight with anger.

As she entered the living area, her eyes quickly scanned the room and found Cole, standing by the fireplace. She inhaled quickly, seeing the same fire she had witnessed last night burning in his eyes. She gave him a weak smile and suddenly she froze as recognition hit her. He was her rescuer; he was the black wolf who had fought for her. "It was you last night, you stopped him."

She didn't notice the others watching her, she could only stare at him feeling something begin to stir inside. His eyes held her with their smoldering color and an unreadable emotion. She tried to speak but nothing came out of her open mouth, shaking her head to break the spell she tried again. "Cole, I, I want to thank you for jumping to my rescue." There she had said it and she didn't stammer like an idiot.

He cocked his head slightly and gave her a lopsided grin. "You're welcome, again." He knew she caught his meaning when her eyes widened like pools of warm chocolate and her hand fluttered to her throat nervously. "You okay?" He could see a slight change in her but he needed to hear it from her.

"Still a little shook but I'll be better soon enough." She avoided looking at him but smiled weakly at the fireplace.

He took her next smile and burned it into his memory, adding it to the precious collection he kept there. His heart skipped a beat giving him back the hope he desperately needed.

Rebecca blinked finally breaking the spell he had cast and quickly regained her composure. "Rick, sorry I didn't come in myself about this." Taking his offered hand, she focused all her attention on the Peace Chief instead of on the man staring at her behind him.

Rick looked from Cole to Rebecca and back again. He had missed something there but now wasn't the time to comment or ask about it. Glancing at the Elder, he caught the old man's headshake and nodded. Clearing his throat, he turned his attention fully to Rebecca and began gently asking questions about her experience.

When she verified that the brown wolf was indeed Miles Darkwing, Rick kept his head and his tongue. "Are you willing to file a formal criminal complaint against him?"

"If his scaring me half to death and threatening me is enough to press criminal charges, then hell yes." She grinned and sat straighter, determination written all over her face. "It's time someone stood up and put a stop to that little jerk."

"Well there lies the problem. We can get him on the stalking with no problem but as to threatening, I'm not sure I can make it stick." Rick scratched the back of his head. "And all he would get is a slap on the wrist and another warning from the tribunal." He looked to the Elder for confirmation. "Unfortunately the tribunal is the highest law we have. And none of them or their families has been harassed by Darkwing so they don't understand."

Cole rolled his eyes and growled softly as his frustration grew. "He can't be allowed to keep this up Rick. If I hadn't jumped in when I did he would have attacked." He could still see Darkwing hunkered down, ready to spring. "If I had been even one moment later we would have been hunting him down for assault or murder."

Rick hadn't realize how close it had been until now with Cole's hackles up. He suddenly turned to Rebecca and searched her face. "Why didn't you protect yourself like Martha did? You're wolf eagle."

Rebecca couldn't hide her reaction from everyone as she sadly looked into Cole's eyes. She saw the same question there but it was softer with some understanding as well. She swallowed a lie and took a rugged breath before admitting the truth. "I can't change and haven't been able to for some time now. I was foolish to let some things fester inside until it all but robbed me of my abilities." She buried her face in her hands and wished she could hide but she felt her spirits embrace her and she dropped her hands to her lap. "I'm ashamed to admit it but plain old fashion human fear stopped me. And by the time the two wolves started challenging each other I knew I couldn't change."

Max cleared his throat and placed his hand on Rebecca's shoulder lending her his silent support. "We don't want this to get out among the people, it could be dangerous. Rebecca is leaving this afternoon to reunite with her spirits. It's been a long time coming and she needs to do this as soon as possible."

Rick arched an eyebrow at the old man. "Isn't that dangerous in it's self? I mean, her taking off alone is just asking for trouble." He could not believe she would take such a risk much less Max allowing it.

Cole cleared his throat and flashed Rick a wicked grin. "I don't have a problem with it but I wasn't asked. Darkwing wouldn't have a clue seeing as you'll have him cooling his heals in your office, explaining himself." He stared at Rebecca trying to read her thoughts but she had closed herself up again.

Looking to Max, he caught his wink and he then understood Max's intentions. Rebecca wouldn't be alone or at least she would think she was. Barely nodding he caught Rick's scowl. "Um, got another thought. Is Rebecca gong to have to go to the office to file the complaint? Because if she does, Darkwing is going to know about it before we want him to." He did not want to tip their hand just yet. He also did not want Darkwing anywhere near her, ever again.

"I could go anyway. It is not as if your office is the only one in the building. He isn't that smart." Rebecca sat forward as another thought came to her. "Or, I could do the paperwork at the clinic. I want to go see Chris." She looked up to her grandfather as he saw what she had in mind. When she felt his gentle hand squeeze on her shoulder, encouraging her, she rushed on. "One of the other Guardians could bring the paperwork there and witness my signature. Isn't that what it takes Rick?" She looked to Rick expectantly. "Rick?"

He cocked his head and gave a slow toothy grin. "Yeah, it's worth the risk. I would have to send Tara, seeing as she has been itching to find an excuse to give Chris a good chewing out. She is a Senior Guardian and she knows the paperwork. And I trust her just as much as the big bad wolf here." Grinning at Cole, he caught a mild scowl and low groan.

Rebecca raised an eyebrow at that comment and Coles face. She thought he had gotten over that name by now, unless he still lived up to it. She wouldn't be one bit surprised if he did.

"I'm past that crap and you know it." Cole growled wishing Rebecca had forgotten his earlier reputation. However, the look on her face told volumes, she still believed he could very well be the bad boy of the community.

"Well seeing as we've concluded our business gentlemen, Cole,' she singled him out purposely, 'I have a few things to do before I go see Chris. Rick, I will be there around one. Is that okay?" She stood and turned to Rick smiling.

"Yeah, that'll work." He grinned down at her, surprised just how calm she was at the moment. He expected her to be like the rest of the women, hysterical, indecisive and in tears.

As she left the room she felt Cole's eyes following her and suppressed a shiver, she stiffened a little but kept walking. Looking down at him from the stairs, she gave him a weak smile and gave a slight wave. "Thanks again Cole. I don't know what would have happened otherwise."

"You are most certainly welcome Becca. " He grinned relaxing a little. He liked this more confident woman, she was almost her old self though she still seemed a little wary but it was a step in the right direction.

Max watched Cole closely and saw the glimmer of hope begin to glow around him and grow in the young man's eyes. He wanted to give that hope a little boost but knew that Cole would need to fight for what he desperately wanted and needed. He personally hoped Cole was up for the challenge ahead of him.

He liked Cole, always had and he admitted to himself that he had personally squelched all the rumors about Cole and Clint's death. Cole was a good man, a little rough around the edges but having a rough life tends to make one so.

Cole shook hands with Max and silently asked for some sign with a raised eyebrow. Max cocked his head and shrugged in answer.

"She's a stubborn child and you can't expect her to accept and absorb the truth over night." He smiled with understanding. "She's got a lot on her table and some of it has to do with you. I can't tell you honestly if she is ready but I think she could use a little shaking up. Rattle those walls a little bit, if you know what I'm saying." Max advised wisely with a sly wink. "She has to let herself re-think and if you're man enough you can push her. Only be ready to catch her when she falls." He looked into Coles eyes and saw the burning there. "North valley, before sunset." He released the young man's hand and stepped back, closing the door in the stunned man's face.

Cole stood in the driveway listening with half an ear to Rick as he ranted in a low voice. His head was spinning with confusion and uncertainty. He appreciated Max's advice and telling him Rebecca's plans. However, he thought she had already exploded last night unless there was more to come. He prayed to the Gods not, she couldn't take another outbreak like the last one.

"Hey man, snap out of it." Rick elbowed Cole to get his attention. "We have to get back and your growls are getting really annoying."

Cole caught himself and coughed to cover another growl. "Sorry, had a rough night and it's catching up with me. Must be feeding…, I mean it must be time to eat…, I mean I need food."

Rick looked sharply at his friend. "You are a mess Cole. If I didn't know any better I would think you've got a thing for that little lady." He saw the warning flash in his friend's eyes and laughed. "Oh man, you have got to be kidding me!" Laughing harder he bent over and slapped his leg. "The big bad wolf is turning into a lovesick pup!"

Cole turned on Rick growling with menace and building annoyance. "Shut the hell up Rick, before I kick your ass."

Rick punched Cole in the arm and swallowed the rest of his laughter. "Come on, we better leave."

"Yeah, before the whole town witnesses your death." Cole clinched his teeth, keeping his emotions under control, barely.

Rebecca peaked from behind the curtain covering the upstairs hall window as the men drove away. She sagged against the wall and let the breath she had been holding out in a rush. She couldn't believe she had actually held her composure as well as she had and she couldn't feel any animosity toward Cole inside.

Cole's presents had rattled her a little but he had also given her his unspoken support. She was confused and she could not figure out why. Her spirits had remained calm while he had been there, lending her their support when she needed it. She at one point thought they accepted him better then her human side. In fact her eagle had done a little joy dance when she first saw him. Eagle told her that she remembered her mate and was elated to be near him once again.

She pushed away from the wall and went in search of her grandfather for a little chat. She found him in his basement workroom, busy working on the dress. She watched him carefully cut thin strips of hide into long narrow fringes with a long bladed knife. She almost jumped out of her skin when he spoke with out turning.

"You handled yourself well earlier." He glanced over his shoulder. "Better then I expected to be honest."

Rebecca entered and perched on a stool at his table. "I surprised myself." Playing with a strip of hide, she peaked at her grandfather's calm face. "I'm confused though. I felt my spirits calm down when I first saw Cole here. Eagle actually did a little dance." She dropped the fringe and took the old man's hand in hers. "Why is that?"

Max stopped cutting and carefully put his knife down, facing her. "I think you need to figure that out for yourself. And it wouldn't hurt to ask your spirits, once you've become whole that is."

"Okay, wise old man." She grinned sheepishly. "I get it, one step at a time." She shrugged and took a deep breath

Sitting beside the hospital bed a few hours later she watched Chris as he tried to fight the sedation. "Hey Chris, don't fight it."

"I hurt so much,' he grumbled weakly as he clutched at the sheets. "I want to talk to you but I'm too tired and I can't think straight."

"We have plenty of time for that later, when you gotten some rest and you're feeling better." She whispered softly as she gently rubbed his temple. "Go to sleep Chris, you'll be better for it." She watched his eyes close slowly as he began to relax.

The swelling as slowly going down but the bruising was getting darker, more pronounced against his pale skin. He would have a seriously crooked nose from now on but he would heal. The nurse had told her that his sinus cavity had taken a nasty blow but they didn't believe he would need surgery to repair it. She admitted that if he hadn't been in his animal form he could have died from the assault.

She shuddered, thinking of what could have happened. She could see a faint similarity between his attack and Clint's accident. They had both been alone in a remote area but Chris had somehow survived his attack. She had known Chris since they were kids with only a year separated them though Chris had been more Clint's friend more then hers. She looked on Chris as part of her extended family and would do anything to protect him. She hadn't been able to help Clint when he died but she could help Chris somehow making it up to Clint.

She still wanted to get whoever had attacked Chris and return the pain that he was going through, a hundred fold if she had the chance. Hearing the door suddenly softly whoosh open behind her, she spun around surprised.

Seeing Tara Willow Song tiptoe in, she released her held breath and sagged in her chair. Putting a finger to her lips she waved the Guardian in. "He's finally resting,' she whispered when TJ reached the bed. "He's still in so much pain."

Tara swallowed convulsively glancing around. "I spent a few hours here early this morning before getting off duty. I'm here on a special assignment."

She saw the woman's eyes soften as they searched the sleeping man's face. She could see the worry and anger flash in TJ's eyes and reassured her softly. "He'll be okay, ya know."

"I know but I wonder if he's going to survive me when he's released." TJ hissed quietly as her green eyes grew a shade darker. "We warned him to be extra careful but like all young men, he thinks he's invincible." Stepping closer she gently slid a finger down his relaxed arm. "Such a pig headed fool."

Chris gave a moan and turned his head from his cousin's voice though he didn't wake, he frowned as if he heard her.

Rebecca rose from her chair and quietly pushed it to TJ. "Why don't you sit with him while I do the paperwork?" Pulling the woman down she took the envelope with her other hand. "He knows you're here so think nice thoughts otherwise you'll upset him."

TJ nodded, keeping her eyes on his lax face. "I'll try."

Walking to the foot of the bed and the adjustable table there, she opened the seal of the thin envelope and quickly scanned the prepared statement and found another one pertaining to the incident on the south road. Satisfied with Rick's work she caught TJ's attention.

TJ stood and watched as she signed and dated at the appropriate places. Taking Chris's chart she turned it over and put the reports on it for TJ's signature. Once done she slipped the paper work back into the envelope and resealed it. "Okay," she whispered, as she began to relax knowing that it was official and done with. "All set. Are you going to stick around?"

TJ shook her head. "I'm under orders to get this back on the boss's desk, ASAP. I'll be back to check on him later though."

Rebecca watched TJ's face soften a little.

"I don't want him waking up and find no one here with him."

She smiled knowingly understand TJ's concern for her cousin. "He'd appreciate it." Gathering her bag, she quietly slipped out of the room with TJ and shook her hand when they parted in the hall.

Leaving the hospital, she decided that she'd take the long winding way home as she slid her windbreaker off. Chris's room had been chilly and she noticed the heat once she had left the building and welcomed it. Looking up to the sky, she couldn't see a cloud anywhere though it smelled like rain.

Before she could reach the end of the clinic walk, she felt like she was being followed and slowly looked over her shoulder to see Cole, striding towards her with his long legs. Taking a deep breath, she turned and planted her hands on her hips. "Why are you following me?"

"No. I'm not following you, I'm chasing you." Grinning he glanced around before clearing his throat. "Honestly?"

"That would be refreshing." Shaking her head, she rolled her eyes. "And just for your information, I don't think I want you chasing me."

Catching up with her, he took her arm and led her across the street. "Ouch."

"Cole, just because you came to my rescue last night doesn't give you the right to follow me around." Slipping her arm from his hand she side stepped a little girl on her tricycle. She wasn't comfortable with him touching her, making her forget even for a moment that she was still angry with him.

"I wanted to tell you that Miles blew a gasket at us and he's swearing up and down it was all a joke. He said he was just funning you." Shoving his hands in his pockets, he looked around again. "He says that he recognized your truck and thought it would be a fun way to welcome you home."

"That's a crock!" Running the thin braid that she wore on her left side, through her fingers, she scowled. "I've only had the truck for three months and I haven't been home for over a year. He's lying through his teeth."

"Hang on, there's more." Watching her, he wondered how long she was going to keep wearing the mourning braid. And her playing with it was like a slap across his face, reminding him of the past. "He changed his story when TJ came in and dropped your statements on Rick's desk."

"Oh this has got to be good." Sniffing she plopped down on the bench and kicked off her shoes. "Well, let me have it."

"Rick had already given him a week's suspension for the stunt on the road, which got him to yelling. But when Rick opened the envelope and handed the complaint about last night to Miles, Miles started screaming his head off." Sitting next to her, he leaned back and tried to hide his laugh. "He said something to the effect that you had called him moments before asking him to meet you. He had the guts to say that you had invited him to a tail chase."

"EXCUSE Me!" Hissing she jumped to her feet and turned towards the Council building. She looked like she was ready to give that jerk a piece of her mind and a swift kick where he would never forget. "Wait till I get my hands on that little jerk!"

"Whoa there, Becca." Grabbing her wrist, he jerked her back down to the bench roughly. "Rick calmly informed him that there is no way, seeing as you just left the council meeting with me."

"Which is a lie," grumbling she continued playing with her braid. "What did he say when he was told you witnessed his threatening posture?"

"He said something about my mother and flipped me off. Then he said he quit and stormed out before we could stop him." Pinching the bridge of his nose, he gave an exasperated sigh. "He's disappeared. But what worries me is that he threatened to get even with you for ruining his life and being a witch."

"He wouldn't dare do it. He has to know the Guardians wouldn't allow it." Swallowing nervously she looked around. "Would he?"

"He was overheard saying he was going to get even with you if it was the last thing he did for messing up his life." Warning her, he grabbed her shoulder to stop her from jumping up again. "That's the reason I'm here, I'm escorting you home"

Sitting back, she felt his anger come at her, in hard waves. "Okay, I believe you but that doesn't give you the right to follow me."

"Becca, damn it, I'm responsible for this happening." Throwing up his hands, he leaned closer to her. "And it is my right to protect you."

"It's your duty as a Guardian, not your right." Hissing at him, she couldn't tell if she was getting angry with him or herself. "I hasten to point out that you don't have that right anymore."

"I have every right Becca, that scar on your neck proves it." Touching the scar, she felt the flutter under it and his finger. "We staked our claim therefore you're ours to protect."

"Don't use that to justify this, Cole." Warning him, she backed away from him, pushing his hand away and glanced around. "It's not fair."

"Who said anything about being fair? You're mine. Your spirits are ours and ours belong to you. You belong to me." Growling down at her, he missed the flash of her hand; he only felt it as it crossed his cheek sharply.

"You lost that right four years ago Cole." Whispering she backed away from him. "When it is all said and done, you left for whatever reason." Jumping from the bench, she slid to the side, away from his reaching hand as she shook her head. "I think that's what hurt the worse. You broke that promise to us."

"I explained that last night." Going after her and grabbing her hand, he pulled her to a stop again. "And you know that you can't just call off a staking claim. Unless your spirits are in agreement and I don't think they would do that."

"You have no idea what they want and don't presume you do!" Raising her voice, she tried to push him away with her free hand.

"Becca, do you even know what they want? When was the last time you spoke to them?" Pulling her close he caught the sudden flash of anguish in her eyes before she turned her head away. "How long Becca?"

"None of your damn business." Hissing in anger, she struggled to get her hand free of his tight grip. "What I do is none of your business, Cole."

"It is when I have to come to your rescue."

"I didn't ask you too." Yelling she struggled against him until he released her. Catching a sob in her throat, she turned and covered her mouth.

"Becca, I'm sorry." Reaching out to her, he felt her put a wall up with enough physical force that his hand bounced off of it. "I shouldn't have asked. But I'm worried about you."

"I'll be fine. Just let me go." Walking away quickly she held her hand out behind her. "Don't follow me, please."

Watching her leave, he ground his teeth and called himself every kind of bastard he could think of. He had thrown up her currant disability in her face, unfairly. He was right when he told her she belonged to him and he did have the right to worry about her. She didn't understand just how unbalanced Miles had been when he left and it could prove to be dangerous for her now.

Chapter 4

Rebecca paused half way up to the meadow and took in the breathtaking view. She could still see snow on the opposite mountain and knew it would be weeks before it melted away. She could feel spring in the air and it smelled heavenly. Hugging herself, she felt some restlessness inside and realized she had better get to the meadow quickly. "Hang on old friend, almost there and then you can come out."

She reached the meadow quickly by running most of the way, pushed by her growing need to become free again. She wasn't as winded or tired as she thought she would be by the time she reached the clearing. She felt just the opposite to tell the truth, invigorated and feeling very much alive.

Stowing her light pack next to the large boulder to her left, she looked around to make sure she was completely alone. Sensing only the natural wild life, she slowly disrobed in the center of the meadow. Feeling the cool air against her skin, she sighed as if she was finally free and stretched her hands to the heavens.

Kneeling in the middle of the meadow, she let herself relax and let earth's own heartbeat speak to her. Concentrating on that ancient heartbeat, she soon felt her own heart slow to match the earths and became part of the earth. She could feel the mountains stretch to the sky and oceans caress earth's skin. She could hear the different wild life walk or run across her and she could feel man as it ignored her. Sighing deeply she blocked out man's indifference, tuning into the mother herself.

She patently knelt, waiting for the caged wolf to notice it was finally free to emerge but nothing happened. She sent coaxing thoughts to her spirit of open running room and complete freedom but it remained inside, pacing back and forth in agitation as it snarled at her. Once it even savagely snapped at her when she called to it using her name for it.

She remembered breaking into a run from the diner days before she left for Arizona. The heart breaking calls of someone had tore through her, driving her to find solace in her apartment. She remembered slamming the door behind her, as she tried to keep her cries inside but both of her spirits had pushed to have their voices heard for the first time in a very long time. Sliding down to the floor, she had let out a haunted keen that shook the windows and bounced off the walls. Both spirits lent their pent up anger, sorrow, understanding and the loneliness of the other eagle's cry with her own. All three let four years of locked up emotions out simultaneously for the first time. Laying against the door her human side shed the long held tears her spirits couldn't and together they shared it all.

After trying every possible way she could think of to encourage her wolf to come out, she began to panic as scalding tears began to run down her face. Gulping in the pure mountain air she quickly worked to calm herself, knowing her agitation was only making it worse. As she steadied herself, she remembered the song she sang in her dreams.

Raising her hands to the sky and closing her eyes, she began softly singing in time with earth's heartbeat. As she gently swayed back and forth, she felt herself really relax and slowly she noticed the change begin with the changing of her voice. The singing turned into low vocalizations that then turned into short lived groans.

It was slow process, slower then was normal but it was to be expected after such a long time and for the first time in her life, it has excruciatingly painful. It was almost as if her wolf was punishing her for keeping it caged inside for so long as it savagely clawed it way out once she knew she had her freedom. Becca threw her head back and cried out when her arms and legs elongated slowly. Her face took on the snout of her wolf and her cry turned into a howl of pain and anguish.

When she had completely changed she lay on the grass and panted until she no longer felt caged or the pain. She rejoiced as everything faded and gave a bark of joy, putting the pain behind her embracing the exaltation of being a wolf.

Opening her eyes she saw the meadow in a new light, everything had an aura shining brightly around it as things became sharper, more defined. Rolling in the old grass and kicking her legs in the air, she groaned in pleasure, ridding herself of the terrible itch on her back and then sighed when it was finally relieved.

Rolling to her feet, she sniffed the air again then took off in a flash of pent up energy and speed. She ran in circles then crisscrossed the meadow only to drop to her stomach and take a small pause. When the breeze blew across her back, she jumped up and did it all again, this time taking time to sniff the grass and flowers until she picked up a faint old and out of place trail. Something did not smell right, something that did not belong here.

Following the trail to the trees, she thought she recognized the scent and gave a small growl in disgust. It had to be marijuana, pot by the stink and the twitch in her nose. Finding a patch of freshly turned earth, she slowly circled it cautiously. When she began to dig, she sent dirt flying in every direction.

Before too long she found a large black plastic garbage bag and inside it, she found individual foil wrapped bundles in smaller baggies. Trying to pulling it out she shook the bag like a dog worrying a rope toy, moving it closer to the surface a little at a time. Once it broke free from its hiding spot, she dragged it away from the hole and saw that the bag was of substantial size. Circling it, she cautiously sniffed it again and sneezed hard enough to hit her snout on the ground, making her yip at the stinging contact.

Oh yeah, she thought, definitely someone's stash of illegal drugs.

Rubbing her snout against some fallen pine needles, she rutted around until she got the smell off her and out of her sinuses. Keeping a safe distance, she noticed more of the freshly turned earth. Cautiously sniffing each one, she knew that she hadn't come across a personal stash but a substantial cache of big trouble. Moreover, all of it would bring no good to her community.

Pacing back and forth, she became agitated as realization hit her that all of this could bring her world, her people and their way of life to an end with a resounding crash.

Spinning away, she left the woods and made for the meadow again, wanting to think with out the drugs staring her in the face. She needed to clear her head so she could figure out what to do about it all.

Sitting behind his desk, staring off into space, Cole finally came to the only conclusion, that like it or not, Becca would have to accept being under his personal protection. In addition, if it meant that they would have to have another screaming match to get it into her stubborn head, then so be it. Jumping to his feet, he called good-bye to Rick in his office. "I've got to take care of some personal business. I'll see you in the morning."

"G' night, Cole." Rick waved absently as he looked over some paperwork. "Tell Rebecca she did the right thing when you catch up with her."

Leaving the office after putting his weapon in lock up, he grinned to himself knowing it was going to be interesting when she saw him up there waiting for her. They were going to have this out for the last time, where there would be no interruptions and no witnesses. It was way past time to face each other and the pain they both carried inside. And he was not going to let her run this time.

Making the hike in record time, he heard such a howl of anguish that the hair on his arms stood up. "Oh god, Becca." Crying out hoarsely he ran until he heard a loud bark of joy coming from the meadow far above him. Slowing to a walk, he knew she had made the change and was fine for now. He was tempted to change and join her but knew that would be pushing his luck. Taking his time he decided to let her have the time to get some of the pent up energy out of her system before he joined her.

Cole sat at the southern end of the meadow next to the bag and patiently waited for her to return. He knew she would be able to smell him well before she saw him, which was a good way to start things. She would either have enough time to decide if she was going to greet him or challenge him for the right to be here. Just because she was a she-wolf didn't mean she couldn't fight for the right to be in the meadow.

He enjoyed sitting there just soaking in the breeze, the air and the view. It was a balm to his troubled soul, rolling mind and pounding heart.

When he caught sight of Becca in her wolf form, his breath caught in his chest and his heart gave a deafening thud. She was glossy, ebony black, sleeker than he remembered and breath taking beautiful. He had not ever forgotten her like this but now he saw her with new eyes. Her fur was that dark, dark black with golden eyes that gave a hint of being truly gold. She carried herself with pride and majesty as she slowed from a lope to a halting walk.

But her eyes held something he never saw before and it actually frightened him a little. There was anxiety, unbridled fury in her glowing eyes and the way she walked towards him, he could tell she wasn't happy.

He held himself very still, fearing she would challenge him because she was mad he was there, following her again.

Becca watched Cole as she slowly and cautiously crossed half of the meadow, pausing to sniff the air. She could smell him since he was openly sitting upwind of her. He smelled strong but at ease, non-threatening and male. His maleness screamed at her making her realize he was the only one who could ever call to her like this.

Sitting and staring at him not blinking, she wondered why he was in her territory and why he was returning her stare back in challenge. She cocked her head slightly listening to his shallow breathing and his heartbeat quickening a little. Turning her back to him, she ignored the feelings he was awakening inside and knew he wouldn't approach as she slowly shifted to her human form.

Keeping her back to him, she picked up her clothes and dressed as if he wasn't watching. "You sure are brave coming here Cole." Calling over her shoulder as she buttoned her shirt, she hid the trembling of her hands. "Was it Grandda or Rick who sent you to spy on me this time?"

Cole cleared his throat before he could trust himself to speak normally. The view of her bare back before it was covered by her hair did a number on him, it made him think of the last time he had seen it, years ago. He remembered spending a long time just making love to it, showering it with kisses and caresses, making her sigh and moan as he took his time worshiping it.

Shaking his head, he forced himself to stick to the here and now. "They didn't ask me but your grandfather kind of told me this morning." He quickly shifted on the rock, hiding his reaction to her before she could turn around.

She slapped her leg in annoyance and ground her teeth. "I don't need a babysitter Cole. I'm a big girl now." Crossing her arms across her chest, she looked up at the darkening sky and blew out an exasperating breath. When were they all going to learn that she didn't want anything to do with Cole Sun Wolf?

"Yeah, I've noticed that." Slowly standing he began walking towards her with measured steps. He warned himself that she may have let him stay in her territory but that did not mean she would allow much else, especially when he had publicly and verbally claimed her as his earlier. But Gods he wanted to touch her, breathe her in, capturing her scent again. "I'll leave you alone if you really want me to."

She shrugged as she felt him stop right behind her. "It's a free country, this land belongs to everyone,' she grumbled. Looking over her shoulder, she gave him a weak nod. "You're welcome to stay."

He let out a soft breath and returned the nod. "Thanks." He couldn't stop his hands from shaking as her scent filled him and the longing to touch her grew. Laying his right hand on her left shoulder, he turned her to face him. "Are, are you okay?"

Damn, he was stuttering like a teenager. And when she looked up to him with that smile, he had to swallow hard to keep his groan in. Her whole face was glowing, her eyes were full of life and the dimple in her cheek deepened. "Never mind, I can see that you're better then okay."

"Oh, Cole,' she laughed loudly. "I feel fantastic! Running free, hearing the world and feeling earth's heartbeat." She laughed harder and spun away. She continued spinning, arms wide and her hair flying out behind her. "It's beautiful!' she yelled throwing her head back. Suddenly she stopped and stared at the setting sun until her eyes burned.

"I almost couldn't do it,' she whispered, shaking her head as she remembered the beginning. "I tried and tried for a long time but nothing happened. I begged and pleaded but she only paced in agitation. Then I remembered a dream and I started to sing. I felt myself begin to change, slowly." Taking a shaky breath, she went on. "I sang in time with earth's heartbeat and my own. That is what finally set my spirit free but when she came out it hurt so much. It was almost like she was paying me back for keeping her locked inside for so long."

Cole watched her face as it reflected her experience, the panic then the remembered pain and then her face changed to the look of wonder. He had seen the wonder in countless faces of the teenagers who had changed fully for the first time. In a split second so many emotions cross an emigrants face. There is fear, panic then bewilderment and awe. "I heard it while I was coming up."

Rebecca's face beamed as she hugged herself, remembering how it felt to be free. "But I did it! My wolf came out to play and run, completely free." Reaching out she laughed. "I swear it was almost as good as the first time I changed."

He could not help but laugh with her and he snatched her hand when she gave him a big smile. He felt her jubilation flow into his hand like an electric shock, running from his hand up his arm to his very core. His heartbeat quickened again and he saw that she felt it too. "Becca," he groaned as he slowly pulled her towards him.

Rebecca saw the fire in his eyes and felt the heat building inside him. She could not resist that heat, feeling it draw her in, beckoning her. Stepping closer she slid her free hand up his stomach to his heart. As its beat quickened she bit her bottom lip as a shiver ran up her spine. Curling her fingers into the tight pectoral muscle, she searched his face.

She could see he was struggling to control himself but the fire in his eyes told her he was close to giving in. Blinking she took that last small step, sliding her hand up to his neck and laid her head against his chest. Sighing she gave in to her spirits demand and the small voice whispering from her heart.

Cole froze, afraid he would wake from this dream only to find that he was alone again. For so long he had dreamt of holding her like this, gently with no fear of reprisal. Releasing her hand, he slowly slid his hands on to her slender hips.

Pulling her against him, he slowly lowered his head, giving her a chance to deny him if she wanted.

Seeing her acceptance and her own need in her eyes, he groaned as he took her mouth hard. His hunger demanded to be sated but his appetite didn't want him to be gentle, they demanded he take everything, now. His hands slid up her sides as their kiss deepened and his fingers dug into her tiny waist.

Rebecca curled her fingers around his neck trying to pull him in closer, wanting to feed on his hunger. She darted her tongue against his, teasing him, ignoring the small voice in the back of her mind telling her she was crazy. She didn't want to let this end and she needed to feel him again after all these years.

His groan from deep inside him pushed her harder, she slowly ground her self against him, telling him she wanted more. It was as if a switch had been turned on inside her and she began pulling at his shirt, desperate to get it off him.

Cole felt the change and he pulled away, breaking the heated kiss. "Becca, hang on a sec." He pushed her away just enough to look down into her glazed eyes. He saw the want, the need and the passion there and growled softly. "Tell me to stop now while we still can."

She shook her head slowly as she pulled his head down and lightly ran her tongue across his lower lip. When he didn't respond, she nibbled at his upper lip. "No,' she rasped, continuing the nibbling building the pressure. "Don't stop."

As he ground his lips on hers, she surrendered completely as he took control. She felt his hand cup her breast through the thin shirt and her sensitive nipples responded quickly.

Cole slid his lips along her jaw and down to her neck. He found the jugular and gently nipped at the small scar there. His eagle had made it four and a half years ago, staking his claim. When her knees buckled, he wrapped his arms around her and held her up, against him. Finding the muscle between her neck and shoulder, he latched on and gently bit her.

At her small cry, he realized he had found one of her erogenous zones and slowly released her, only to bite down again and again. When her head tipped back, he bit hard, gnawing on the lax muscle.

Rebecca felt herself explode at his gnawing and clutched at his shoulders, digging her nails into his tight muscles. When the last wave crashed through her, she cried out his name and felt herself go completely limp in his arms.

Chapter 5

Cole gently picked her up and cradled her in his arms. He never had a woman respond like that before and it frankly amazed him. He carried her to the center of the meadow and laid her on the tall grass and wild flowers. Lying beside her, he brushed the hair from her face gently, watching her as she continued to shudder.

As her eyes fluttered open, she blushed and grinned impishly. "I bet you can't do that again.' she whispered huskily. She ran a finger over his bottom lip, seeing the gash had opened and oozed a little blood. She hissed knowing it must sting like crazy.

Cole caught her finger between his teeth and ran his tongue over the tip of her finger. Seeing her eyes widen he took another finger between his teeth and slid his tongue between them slowly, making her breathe in short gasps. Sliding her fingers out, he held her hand as he laid small soft kisses across her palm down to her wrist. He could feel her pulse quicken under his lips and he lightly ran his tongue over the vein making her groan.

When she reached up with her other hand, he took it and repeated the process until she was panting. He pulled her arms over her head and she gave a wicked chuckle when he raked his eyes down her stretched body. When he rolled on top of her, she barely felt his weight on her hips and she saw his own wicked grin.

He surprised her when he took both of her wrists in one hand and slowly wrapped some of her hair around them. Now she was bound and unable to free them without pulling her hair out.

Cole gently skittered his fingers down the insides of her arms, barely touching her. When he reached her ribs, she found herself panting harder. Arching her back, she silently begged him to touch her aching breasts but when his hands stopped at her waist, she whimpered.

He slowly ran his hands over her stomach watching her silently plead with him. Shaking his head, he slowly moved to the first button of her shirt and exposed her stomach. Moving down until he was able to rest his head there, listening to her heartbeat and her breathing. Nibbling around her belly button with his lips, he chuckled as she arched her back at the surprise contact. Taking his time, he slowly exposed another inch and ran his mouth over it. After agonizing minutes of his torture she was moaning and begging for more. As he released the last button, she was begging him not to stop as she twisted under him. Slowly pulling her shirt open, she gasped as the fabric slide across her very sensitive nipples.

Sitting up he laid a finger against her lips when she whined in protest. Pulling his shirt off, he tossed it aside never breaking eye contact. Her heaving chest caught his attention and he watched fascinated as her nipples hardened.

He couldn't help but growl and quickly bent taking the left nub between his lips. Scrapping his teeth across it, he slid his hands under her and wrapped his arms around her, pulling her closer. He drew her breast deep into his mouth, making her cry out when he gently tugged. He quickly released her moving to her right nipple, taking only the hardened nub between his teeth. As he gently chewed, she gasped then moaned repeatedly.

Slipping his right hand down her body, he found the already moist junction of her legs. Pushing her short leg aside, he quickly slipped his hand in, cupping her heated sex.

Rebecca began tossing her head from side to side, as she felt her body respond to his searching fingers. When he found her slick entrance, she cried out as he slid a long finger in deep. He slowly pulled out, adding a second watching her as he slowly entered her again. He felt his control slipping, feeling his need beginning to crest to the unbearable.

She felt a sudden breeze blow across her super heated skin and whimpered as Cole rolled off her. She blinked rapidly to clear the haze to see Cole removing his jeans and tossing them to the side. When he returned he unwound the hair freeing her hands and helped her slip her shirt off. He gently pushed her down and then slid her shorts down her slender hips and legs.

She reached up to lock her hands around his neck as he moved up her body and held himself over her, hovering. She tried to pull him down but he kept his arms locked, giving her the opportunity to stop him if she wanted. She felt his knee push her legs further apart when she continued to hold up her arms and she rubbed herself against his muscled thigh showing him her urgency.

His eyes locked on to hers as he slowly lowered himself until he was nestled against her. As he slowly ground his hips, he knew the pressure he was applying could send her over the edge easily. When he saw her breath become rapid, he repositioned himself and thrust in. Gritting his teeth, he pushed until he was deeply buried inside stretching tight muscles. He held himself still while her muscles constricted and relaxed in mild spasms as they grew accustom to him again.

Groaning Rebecca threw her head back feeling him grow larger then she remembered, filling her completely. Feeling him shift slightly she felt him pull her legs over his arms then clamping them between his forearms and biceps as he lowered his arms, resting his arms on the ground beside her body.

Cole buried his face in her neck feeling her throbbing jugular against his cheek. Slowly he withdrew and returned to the slick tight heaven that was her, feeling her hands grasping at his back.

As he continued building the tempo, he began laying soft kisses on her neck. When she started matching his movements, he began softly biting her exposed neck, thrusting into her harder. As she began a long, loud moaning he let go of his hard held control and drove him self in deeper then ever before. When she screamed out her climax, he bit but did not break the skin on her shoulder as his own released exploded inside her.

Rebecca never felt his teeth scrapping her skin only extreme pleasure and an explosive orgasm that left her drifting in star-studded darkness. Holding Cole tightly she shuddered several times as she tried to catch her breath. Feeling him return the shudders, she tightened her muscles, making him gasp in surprise.

She gave a weak giggle when he convulsed again. Running her nails down his muscular back, she felt his muscles ripple in response.

Raising his head, she saw that his eyes had taken on the golden brown of his wolf and her breath caught in her throat. She realized that at some point in their lovemaking, his canines had lengthened and she had enjoyed the enhanced roughness.

He felt his teeth slowly change back and gave her a slow wicked grin. "I think you almost turned me inside out." Growling he dropped his head and nuzzled her neck. "I almost couldn't control myself any longer."

She felt his sigh as she slowed her hands at his neck and caught his hair in her fingers. "I'm not mad,' she whispered finding her voice. "You weren't the only one who lost control."

He inhaled deeply taking in her scent mixed with freshly crushed grass, wild flowers and their mingled sweat. He could have stayed this way, lying on top of her, holding her tight against him, forever. However, he knew she would either be crushed or suffocated by his weight before too long. Shifting his body, he pushed himself up, rolled off her, and pulled her against him.

Rebecca laid her head on his shoulder and placed a hand over his still racing heart. Sighing she felt the strong beat under her fingers slowing to a normal rhythm. "Cole, did you come up here because Grandda told you to or because you wanted to?" Raising her head, she stared at him, wanting to hear the truth from him.

Pulling her on top of him, he wrapped his arms around her caressing her back. "I came because I wanted to be sure you were okay. And I wanted to talk to you about something." Tucking her hair behind her ear, he grinned. "But it can wait for another time. I don't want to break this spell you've cast."

"I didn't cast a spell Cole, I just let myself go." Sitting up quickly she straddled his stomach. "I don't know why but I can't fight you anymore Cole. Trust me, I tried and it only hurt me." Taking a deep breath, she continued. "I know that holding in the ugly emotions had almost caused serious damage but I needed it to keep going. When you showed up here, I knew I couldn't fight it anymore. And our lovemaking makes me see that there still might be something between us."

Cole held his breath feeling a 'but' coming. Grabbing her caressing hands, he held her still. "Go on."

She bit her lip and cocked her head. "I'm afraid of you Cole and how you make me feel. You've turned my life upside down twice now and I don't know what to do." She saw his eyes slowly lose that glow from their lovemaking to turn dull and she felt his grip on her wrists loosen.

"I understand Becca, you can't quite let the past go and you don't trust what is between us." He gently pushed her off his stomach and shook his head. "I guess it was too much to hope for." He grabbed his jeans and stood to dress, turning his back to her.

She felt sudden hot tears threaten to spill from her eyes and told herself she was not going to let them fall. "I'm sorry Cole, I don't mean to hurt you. I just don't know what I want right now. So much is happening to me all at once and I feel like I've been caught in a tornado, being tossed from one place to another, one emotion to another." Getting to her feet, she tried to reach out for him. "Please try to understand."

He stepped away, as if letting her touch him would only anger him and he didn't want to be angry. "Oh, I understand Becca, better than you think. You need time to get everything straightened out in your little head. But let me give you a piece of well learned advice." Looking over his shoulder, he saw the tears shining in her eyes and refused to let them move him. "Listen to your heart more this time. It knows the truth and doesn't concern itself with all the, what if's and maybe's."

She saw the pain and anger in his eyes knowing she had caused it with out trying. "No Cole, you don't understand what I'm saying." Crying she stepped closer still reaching out to him. "I need you to understand."

Cole spun, grabbed her by the shoulders and growled, barely containing his growing anger. His eyes glowed as his emotions intensified. "Make me understand Becca because I'm confused as hell right now,' he growled. "At least tell me that what just happened wasn't on a whim or out of gratitude."

She swallowed nervously, not fighting him as she just stood there crying. The words she had intended to say got lost half way to her throat. Shaking her head in frustration she cried harder. "I'm sorry Cole, I don't know where to start."

She watched his eyes go blank as he pushed her away from him as he stepped back. When he walked away, she felt a sharp pain in her heart and in her stomach as if something wanted to go after him. Sobbing, she wrapped her arms around her waist and fell to her knees. She didn't see him hesitate only heard his hoarse voice thick with emotion.

"Come find me when you've got yourself figured out Becca. I have been waiting for you for fours agonizing years. I can't promise I'll wait another four, it would kill me and my spirits."

She knelt in the meadow crying for a long time after he left before she finally moved lying down. The evening air had gotten chilly and there was the strong smell of rain coming on the wind from the west. Hearing the thunder rolling in she rolled to her side and curled into a ball wrapped in her misery. She didn't feel the first raindrops as her mind slowly replayed his words repeatedly. When lightening struck some distance from her, she barely flinched and when the thunder followed a short time later, she rolled to her back.

She just listened to his words telling her he had waited and would wait but not forever. She knew he was right when he told her that her heart knew the truth and it was the wiser.

It told her she needed him as much as she needed air to live and he was the only one her spirits wanted. He had always tried to reach out to her even when he was thousands of miles from her. He was always there in her mind, waiting for her to wake up, behind the door she kept tightly closed but never locked. She remembered when her sensitive ears had picked up the far off cry of either hunting or elated Eagle days before she decided to come home. She had almost stumbled when the cry took on a lost lonely pitch lasting for almost a minute, giving an involuntary gasp. That cry ripped straight through her, it had been a heart ripping cry and as it faded she felt more alone then at any other time in her life. Her reaction was completely surprising to her, hysteria and the release of years of anguish from her lonely spirits and heart.

Pushing herself up she realized that she still loved him and he was the one she had always heard calling in her dreams. He had been calling out for his mate, and she had foolishly ignored it out of pride, stupidity and fear.

She had never known Cole to lie to her or anyone else for that matter and yet, she had doubted him when he had told her he had left a letter for her, explaining why he left. All those unopened letters she had received through the years proved doubly that he had cared. She was the one who had ran, not him. She had ran for so long that she had actually left her heart behind and coming home she found that it was still here, waiting for her to claim it.

Fighting herself for so long had done nothing but make her miserable now. her spirits had all but turned their backs on her and they were at one point ready to abandon her. They were a little restless but they forgave her and that she was loved and they where here to stay. They sent her images of calm and peace, helping her to understand they would never again threaten to leave her.

Feeling as if the pouring rain was cleansing her, she stood limply as the water soaked her. Finding her scattered clothes, she dressed quickly in the growing darkness. As she buttoned her shirt, she realized she had better find shelter somewhere because the storm was getting worse and she knew she couldn't make it home before it came to full power.

Snatching up her backpack, she remembered the old lodge west of the meadow hoping that it would keep her somewhat dry and safe until this passed. Making her way carefully she started shivering as the temperature began to drop quickly. She had not dressed for this weather and she hadn't brought so much as a windbreaker to protect herself.

She barely caught herself before she slipped to the muddy ground, dropping her bag and clinging to a sapling to catch her breath. She felt the scrap on her temple and wiped at the sting to find blood on her fingers. The wind had become stronger whipping her clinging wet hair into her face and against the wound as she tried to get her bearings.

Relying on her wolf senses, she realized too late that she had passed the old lodge a while ago and groaned. Pulling her hair into a bundle, she quickly tucked as much of it as she could in to her shirt, shivering as it clung to her back, cold and dripping.

Looking around she decided her best bet was to keep heading southwesterly, down the mountain instead of backtracking up and closer into the storm. If she had missed the lodge once, she could very well miss it again, wasting precious time.

Moving from tree to tree, she slipped and slid on the old pine needles that blanketed the ground along with the old leaves from the Aspens didn't help her footing. She fell several times, skinning her hands and knees, on fallen limbs and loose rocks, knowing she was getting tired and clumsy with the cold, fighting against the wind.

When a lightening bolt struck a tree a few yards from her she screamed in surprise and began to run, tapping into her spirits strength. She felt limbs whipping at her body and head as she tried to dodge the smaller swaying trees. Running down hill was dangerous but staying out in this storm was much worse. The longer she stayed on the mountain the more danger she was going to be in once the center of the storm hit.

Cole sat before the fireplace tossing in small sticks, thinking of how he had treated Becca. He could have given her the chance to explain but he suspected he would not have like what she would say. He had heard her gut wrenching sobs but it did not stop him from leaving her there, alone with her misery. He knew his words had been rough enough but truthful and his next ones could have very well put an ending to everything, permanently.

Grabbing his untouched beer, he downed half of it in annoyance. He really wanted to open that bottle of Beam he had spied in the cabinet over the fridge but did not move to get it. He had been down that road once before and it had not helped him.

The fire kept his attention with its dancing flames as they moved like she had earlier, sensuously erotic, enticing him to come get closer to be burned again. Lying back on the hardwood floor groaning and he covered his face with his arms. Damn, he needed to stop thinking about it.

Hearing the thunder and wind rattle the windows as it drove the rain in sheets across the land, he sat up catching the lightening as it flashed behind the house. He laughed when his wolf grumbled in response, he knew the feeling too well. The storm outside and the one inside him were very similar in many ways, angry and making the world know it was there. Seeing a lightening bolt hit just up the mountain he closed his eyes and jumped when he heard an explosion just before the thunder rolled over his head.

He slowly got to his feet and walked to the back window to count the seconds between thunder and lightening. Leaning his hands on either side of the window, he counted to five when the lightening struck to the right, lighting up the dark sky. He leaned closer after his eyes adjusted from the brilliant flash, squinting out through the driving rain pressing his nose against the cold window. He could barely see just beyond the opposite side of the garden fence and saw a silver wolf standing there. It stared at him with glowing eyes across the yard.

Going to the back door, he opened it and stepped out wondering if his mind was playing tricks on him again. The wolf shimmered as if the wind was trying to pull it apart but it remained, never blinking. Cole felt his wolf become instantly agitated, pacing erratically back and forth, telling him something was terribly wrong.

Stepping off the porch, he watched the ghost wolf as it stood and faced up the mountainside. When it looked back at him over its shoulder, he heard it in his head as he stepped towards it.

"Come."

Cole jumped off the porch to run after it but the wind blew against him, trying to push him back to the house. He could barely stand as he struggled to follow the wolf, never closing the gap between them. He didn't feel the rain as it lashed against him but it caused him to squint as it burned his eyes. He lost sight of the silver shimmer once as he struggled to catch up tripping over a downed tree limb.

It suddenly reappeared at his side when it looked like he was going to fall to his knees. "Change,' it commanded staring deep into his eyes. 'Change before it is too late."

Cole nodded and called his wolf out as he undid his soaked jeans. He felt himself shimmer as he dropped to his hands and knees, shifting with ease and speed. Once fully changed he raced after the ghost, easily keeping pace. The wind and rain did not fight him now.

They raced up the mountain towards the last lightening strike and Cole's keen ears picked up a weak cry that was not the wind whipping through the trees. He caught the smell of burnt wood in the wind and another terrified cry for help.

He finally saw Becca, caught under the fallen tree and skid to a stop. The tree had been hit by lightening half way up, causing it to split in half and she had been pinned by it when it fell. She was trying to get the heavy trunk off her knees but it was too big and heavy for her to move by herself. He approached her from the left trying not to surprise her with his presence but she only saw the ghost wolf on her right. He saw her shivering and her eyes go wide with fear.

He stepped beside her rumbling low in his chest until she slowly turned her head to him. "Cole, help me. I can't get free.' she stammered as another chill raced through her. "I'm so cold."

He nodded and moved to where her legs were pinned looking over the possibilities. Carefully he began digging the wet dirt away from her and under the tree. He dug carefully not wanting to claw her already bleeding legs causing her any more pain. He was so engrossed in his mission that he did not realize that the ghost had faded away.

Rebecca gasped as the silver wolf disappeared, calling out her brother's name and reached for it to come back. She felt his words in her heart when the wind continued to howl. "You're safe now Becca, you're safe."

She started struggling when she felt Coles wet paws under her knees, pulling away more dirt but she was too exhausted. Moaning in frustration she felt helpless to do anything but lay there, making him do all the work. Grabbing at Cole's fur, she pulled at him weakly. "Stop, it is not working. You have to change back and push this off me. It's the only way." She shivered uncontrollably and the wind continued to whip the rain around her. "Please Cole, change back. I don't think I can hang on much longer."

Cole stepped back and let his wolf relinquished control knowing she was right. He couldn't move the trunk as a wolf and digging would take up precious time that she didn't have especially when the dirt was sliding back under her knees.

As he changed, he felt the cold rain against his bare skin and knew time was now critical for them both. He went to the end of the tree and slowly lifted it, gritting his teeth, ignoring the branches whipping at his face. "Move Becca, quick before I lose my grip,' he growled against the wind. "Move back NOW!"

She rolled to her stomach and dragged herself free from under the tree, clawing at the ground pulling her self a few feet beyond it. He could see that her legs were burning as the blood flow returned making her scream out in agony. She had to have heard Cole yelling her name but the exhaustion along with the pain overwhelmed her and she let the blackness take over.

Cole saw her limp sprawled out body and called her name again. Letting the tree fall to the ground with a dull thud, he raced to her side and gently rolled her to her back. He noticed her pale skin around blue lips and felt his fear spur him to move faster. Gathering her in his arms, he moved as quickly as he could without jostling her and headed home. The wind was at his back now but the rain was coming in harder sheets causing him to squint.

Suddenly he saw the silver shimmer before him leading them both to safety. When he stumbled he felt his own strength begin to weaken but felt his energy return when the lights of his house slowly come in sight.

They reached the back gate as another lightening bolt struck near where he estimated they had found Becca. Looking down at the wolf, he shuddered and held her tighter to him. "Thank you."

"Go. " It encouraged him as it slowly stepped back. "Go." It whispered as it slowly faded away.

Feeling Becca shivering uncontrollably in his arms, he took the steps two at a time and kicked the door open. Striding through the house, he headed to the living room and the dying fire. Laying her carefully on the thick braided rug, he quickly checked her pulse and breathing. Her heartbeat was slow but steady, which gave him a small measure of relief. As she shivered again, he tossed several logs on the low fire and stirred the embers until it roared back to life.

Seeing some color slowly coming back to her skin he stood and ripped a horse blanket off the nearest chair and covered her with it. He ignored his own discomfort until he was sure she was getting warm. Letting her rest where she was, he left her to find some clothes and that bottle of Beam. Both of them were both going to need it, sooner or later.

Rebecca felt the heat around her as she slowly opened her eyes to see that a fire was roaring in front of her and she wiggled closer. She felt the coarse blanket around her and held it tightly against her. It smelled of wood smoke, dampness and of Cole.

She sat up slowly feeling very weak and took in her surroundings. She was in Cole's house, out of the storm and safe. Hearing a cabinet close she turned to see him in the doorway holding a bottle and a towel, wearing only low riding jeans.

"Hey,' she whispered weakly. "How did I get here?"

He let out a slow breath as he saw the fire create a red dancing aura around her. He felt that familiar tightening in his groin and swallowed his groan. Not now you idiot, he told himself as he slowly crossed the room to stand over her, not now.

He knelt at her knees, set the bottle down and gently pulled her wet hair from her face. "I carried you here. Almost didn't make it off the mountain when I couldn't see through the rain. But he showed up and led me all the way back here."

He watched her eyes dart to the window and knew she wanted to see him again to prove to herself that he was real. "Yeah, you saw him, same as I did." He sat down and bent a knee, resting his arm on it. He glanced at the window and then back at her. "He showed up after the lightening strike, called me to follow and led me to you." He didn't add that if he hadn't there was no telling what could have happened.

She sighed and shivered again, drawing the blanket tighter around her. "You know that the silver wolf was Clint, don't you?" She barely whispered looking into the fire. "He's been coming to me in my dreams lately but only in the dreams."

"He's been doing the same here." He cleared his throat nervously. Reaching for the bottle, he paused seeing her shaking under the blanket. Twisting the top off he pushed it towards her, nodding. "Here take a belt. It'll help warm you up some." Tipping the neck at her, he grinned. "One belt won't hurt Becca, it'll do you good."

She sighed and snaked her hand out from under the blanket looking as if she was afraid the bottle would bite her. Taking the bottle in her trembling hand, she brushed his fingers and felt the electric shock. Looking up at him through her lashes, she saw him flinch. Bringing the bottle up to her nose, she smelt the alcohol as it burned her nose and hesitated for a moment. Grimacing she took a deep breath and tipped the bottle. Coughing, she felt it burn a path to her stomach. Taking a larger pull, she felt the heat of the whiskey warm her insides a little. Shivering she handed the bottle to him gasping for air, shaking her head.

He sat watching her, seeing more color coming back to her face and nodding once in satisfaction. Her eyes were clearer but still a little dull. Tipping the bottle to his own lips, he let the whiskey burn a path inside before putting it down between them. He could smell the wet blanket and realized she needed to get out of her wet clothes soon or she would be sick later. In addition, he really needed to put some space between them. "I'll get you some dry things to change into." He stood to leave but she caught his hand. Looking down he felt trapped in her glazed eyes. "I'll be right back."

She wanted to say something but the words flew out of her head when he looked at her with a blank face. Swallowing, she nodded and whispered thanks, giving him a small smile. She wanted to tell him she had been wrong and such a fool.

He slowly stepped away, letting his fingers slowly slip from hers. Nodding he turned and ran up the stairs to his room.

Rebecca heard his footsteps on the boards above her and drawers opening then slamming closed. What caught her attention was his low grumbling then a door, quietly slamming shut. She couldn't hear what he was saying because of the howling wind outside but she knew he was upset.

She stared into the fire, sure that he was upset because of her, not that she blamed him any. When the thunder exploded above the house, she almost jumped out of her skin and covered her ears. When the lightening struck right outside the back window she let out a short cry of surprise before hiding her face in the blanket.

Cole swore and headed for the stairs, an old sweatshirt in hand when the lights flickered and then went out. "Damn it,' he yelled when he stubbed his toe on the door jam.

Rebecca pulled herself to the fire and stirred it, encouraging it to burn brighter. "Cole, where are the candles?' she called as she tried to get to her feet. She had not counted on being so weak until her legs refused to cooperate and she found herself back on the floor in a heap. Her knees were killing her and she bit back the tears as she straightened them out from under her.

When she heard him coming down, she looked up to see him carrying a lantern and some clothes. "I seem to have a problem standing." She felt her knees burning and noticed the cuts and bruises for the first time. Hissing she gingerly touched the biggest gash and watched as fresh blood slowly rolled down her leg onto the rug.

He crossed the room and saw her examining her legs as she tried to stop the flow of fresh blood. The feeling that washed over him made him sink to his knees beside her. Setting the lantern down carefully beside her, he gently pushed her hands away so he could see the damage. One cut bleed freely while the others had already began to clot into scabs.

Looking her over he saw she had scratches everywhere and a nasty scrape at her temple. "We better get you cleaned up and dry before you get sick."

He looked at her clinging clothes and saw her blush shyly. "Don't move. I'll be right back."

He left her before he could do something brilliant like pull her into his arms and kiss her senseless. That would have made for a bad situation friend, he told himself as he gathered more towels and the first aid kit from the small bathroom. He found a bowl in the kitchen and filled it with what water he could get from the tap.

He would have to go out and start the generator but first he had to get Becca patched up and comfortable. She was his first priority right now. He found her sitting on the fireplace base, back against the warm stones set in the wall, with her head turned towards the front window, a tear rolling down her cheek as she chewed her bottom lip.

Rebecca couldn't keep her emotions in check any longer. She wanted to tell Cole so much now but she could not find the right words. She wanted to apologize for being weak, for hurting him earlier but she couldn't think straight. Staring out the window, she remembered the look on his face, when he left her in the meadow and Gods it hurt.

Wiping the tear away with a shaking hand she felt him watching her from the dark kitchen and slowly turned towards him. "Sorry, I guess everything is catching up with me." She gave him a weak smile while avoiding his searching eyes

"Yeah, you've been through hell the last few days." He set the bowl close to the fire, to get it warm. "Here, let's get you fixed up and then we'll talk, if you want."

He took a small towel and dipped it into the tepid water. Dabbing at the cuts on her face he noticed she refused to look at him. He felt her flinch as he gently wiped the scrape at her temple. The silence was deafening when she cleared her throat suddenly.

"I stayed in the meadow for a long time, thinking and soul searching. I didn't realize there was a storm on the way and when it picked up I realized I wouldn't make it home before it hit in full force.' whispering she took several deep breaths. "I intended to get to that old lodge but I had passed it before realizing. By then the storm was getting stronger and the lightening struck close to me several times. I panicked and headed down the mountain figuring I could reach some place safe on the edge of town. However, I ran out of luck when that last lightening bolt hit that tree. I got knocked down by the blast and the tree snapped."

Looking at his hands, she shivered. "I was lucky enough to roll side ways before it landed, I don't think I would have survived otherwise."

He bent and wiped a tear from her bruised cheek. "But you did survive and you kept fighting. Life is worth fighting for, no matter what Becca. And you won that fight." He pulled her face up and stared down at her. "You didn't quit and that's all that matters."

"You're right. I also know that I've been fighting for all the wrong reasons lately and it's time I started on the right ones." She cupped his jaw and traced that cut lip. "The right battle has been there all along but I refused to see it until tonight."

He let the towel drop to the floor as he cupped the back of her head, pulling her closer. "You don't have to fight me Becca. There never was a war between us, you know that, don't you?"

She nodded slowly finally warmed inside and out by his simple touch. "I want you Cole, I always have. However, as you said, my head was not letting my heart lead. I am so sorry Cole. I can't tell you how sorry I am." Finally getting the pent up thoughts out into words out she sobbed.

He gathered her into his arms and rocked her as her heart poured out everything it had held under lock and key. He let her tell him about her fears, her anger at herself for not giving him the chance he deserved. Her sobs broke her admission telling him that what she was saying was from deep inside and from her heart. He did not let her go as she sobbed, just held her close encouraging her to let it out.

When she finally exhausted herself and fell asleep in his arms, he carefully picked her up and carried her up to his room. Laying her on his bed he gently removed her clothing noticing the welts and bruises the storm had inflicted on her slender body. He worried about her legs as he saw the knees were badly bruised and swelling. They weren't' broken thank god but they were badly banged up.

He left the room, retrieved the first aid kit, lantern and towels. She laid there in a deep exhausted sleep as he cleaned and dressed her wounds gently. She had moaned as he finished lowering her leg and he almost gave in to the urge to kiss her bandaged wounds. When he slid off the bed, she reached out and caught his pant leg weakly.

"Stay.' she whispered as she struggled to wake. "Stay with me."

He knelt on the bed and placed a chaste kiss on her forehead. "I'll be back in a minute.' he whispered to her as she drifted off back to sleep. "I promise."

He went back downstairs, banked the fire and picked up the clothes that he had brought down for Becca to change into earlier. Checking the doors and windows, he doused the lantern and went back up to her. He wasn't going to let her be alone, never again.

She lay slightly curled up on her side, hair fanning out across the bed behind her. Cole paused before entering knowing she belonged there and he had to find a way to convince and keep her there. Quietly undressing he heard her sigh and mumble. He carefully brushed her hair until it lay beside her and lay down behind her. He didn't want to disturb her as he slowly slid a hand to her hip, watching her sleep. Pulling the sheet over them, he let his head drop on his arm and fell asleep breathing her in.

The next morning Rebecca found herself in a strange bed feeling as if she had been beaten to within an inch of her life. Groaning she remembered the night before and everything that she had been subjected to while she tried to out run the storm. She slowly rolled to her back and sat up stiffly careful not to bend her knees too much. She knew she was naked but smiled when she saw small bandages covering cuts and scraps. She remembered his hands gently tending to her and holding her when she passed out but not how she had gotten in his bed or undressed.

Trying to drawing her knees up, she hissed as they protested with sharp pain. Throwing back the blanket and sheet, she saw the dark bruises across them. Touching them gingerly, she felt that there was a bit of swelling but no serious damage, they were just sore as hell.

Stretching stiff muscles, she glanced at the clock and saw it was actually noon and groaned in disbelief. She figured she had slept a full twelve hours but felt like she could use another twelve before she would feel normal again.

Searching for her clothes, she found just a soft t-shirt of Coles lying across the foot of the bed and slipped it over her head. She couldn't do anything about her hair so she wound it and pulled it over her shoulder. Feeling her shoulder muscle give a sharp twinge, she gently touched it under the shirt. Not feeling any scratches she tried to look but could not see what was causing the soreness.

Hobbling to the mirror hanging on the closet door she pulled the shirt off her shoulder and noticed the bruises left by his teeth. She stared at them with wide eyes remembering when and how Cole had made them while they made love. She also remembered her response at the time and blushed up to her hair roots.

She didn't hear Cole come upstairs or him entering the room but she saw him through the mirror, watching her through half closed eyes. She spun and almost fell when her knees protested their abuse. Recognizing the smoldering fire in his eyes, she felt butterflies in her stomach and heat slowly building lower. "I remember,' she gasped. At a loss for words, again.

"We do too, vividly as a matter off fact." He approached her as if he was stalking prey, cautiously, expecting her to bolt if the chance came. "I think when you offered your neck like you did is what did me in."

She blushed again and slowly pulled the shirt up covering the marks, not realizing the material now drooped low in the front. She felt his eyes slowly slid from her face to her neck, down to her hardening nipples. She self-consciously crossed her arms trying to hide what his actions were doing to her. Moreover, she had to admit he was making her want more of what they had yesterday.

Clearing her throat nervously she fidgeted until he grinned at her. "Cole, I need food. You've provided shelter, first aid and comfort but no food." She looked at his throat instead of looking at his face. She already knew what she would find there but now was not the time. "Cole, food please, before I parish here right before you."

Cole crossed his arms over his chest and laughed wickedly. He looked like he would have gladly continued to keep her captive in his room but when her stomach protested loudly, he relented. "Come on, I can't stand a rumbling tummy in a woman." He let her carefully walk past him, keeping his hands to himself as he followed closely behind her just in case she stumbled.

Rebecca took the stairs one at a time, not trusting her knees completely. When she reached the landing, she was sore as hell, sweating and panting from the excursion. Reaching the couch, she fell on it refusing to go any further as she mopped her face.

Cole slid a pillow behind her and then helped her get into a better position before reaching behind her head. Handing her a bottle of aspirin and another of water he winked. "Figured you would only get this far, before finally giving up."

She sighed and took them, grateful he had thought ahead. "Thanks. I didn't think my knees would hurt so badly." Popping two aspirin into her mouth, she quickly opened the water and took a drink. She drained the bottle realizing she was very thirsty. She felt him lean over her and almost jumped when he traced the bruises with a finger.

"You're going to walk funny for a while but there's no serious damage, as far as I can see." He knelt down behind the couch and folded his arms across the back becoming very serious. "We have a bit of a problem Becca. Well, let's say some problems." He brushed her hair back gently. "The phones and power are out. I found that several old trees are down across the lane and on the main road. And,' he sighed, "I can't get the generator to start."

Becca stared at him in disbelief. "You're saying we're cut off from town, aren't you?" She could tell he was being very honest with her. "What are we going to do? I have to let my folks know that I am okay. I was supposed to be home last night."

"I guess we could hike out of here into town but I honestly don't think you're up to it, not with your knees banged up." He thought of something but instantly dismissed the idea as dangerous.

She caught the flash and the headshake and grabbed his arm. "What? You thought of something, didn't you?"

He shook his head and grimaced. "I was thinking you could change and make your way home but it wouldn't work. Either spirit would be hurt too. You don't need their pain added to yours." Laying his hand over hers, he couldn't hide the growing grin. "Looks like you're stuck here for a day or two, at least."

She narrowed her eyes and then laughed. "You're just loving this, aren't you?" She ruffled his hair until he pulled away. "Big bad wolf has to be nice,' she teased gently. "The proud wolf can't let an injured woman get hurt again so he keeps her in his den."

Narrowing his eyes, he growled wickedly and snapped playfully at her hand. "I bet this big bad wolf can keep you from getting bored." Pulling her up to him, he held her chin still and let her see the fire in his eyes, again he grinned. "Injured or not just remember I bite and you've got a lot of places I haven't bitten, yet." Letting her slip from his arms he stood and left the room listening to her sputter and calling him foul names, laughing.

She wanted to throw something, anything at his retreating back but there wasn't anything close enough to grab. Spying the covered tray on the coffee table beside her, she grinned realizing she had the perfect missile nearby. She changed her mind when she suddenly smelt food coming from it. Carefully pulling the table closer she felt her mouth water and lifted the covers off one at a time.

A full breakfast had been sitting there waiting for her all this time. Snatching a piece of toast, she crammed half of the wedge into her mouth. Chewing quickly she grabbed the orange juice and drank it down with out taking a breath. She ate quickly as if she was starving which she was and before she knew it, the plates were empty. Wiping her mouth, she wished there was more but that knew too much after a full day of not eating could cause problems and maybe embarrassment.

Leaning back, she heard him making noises in the kitchen and wondered what he was doing in there. Jumping at a loud banging, she wondered if he had dropped something important. "Hey Cole,' she called over her shoulder sweetly. "Need a hand in there?"

"No, you just stay put." Popping his head out, he forced a bright smile as he swore under his breath. "I've got everything under control in here." Ducking back into the kitchen, he lowered his voice to keep his mumbling to himself and a lot quieter.

She giggled behind her hand as more banging came from the kitchen followed by several colorful words. Before long, he came out holding a finger in his mouth and looking rather sheepish. She saw faint red marks across his hand and groaned. "What happened in there? It sounded like a battle zone."

Pulling out his injured finger, he held it up for her to see the blister forming. "I fired up the wood stove to make some stew and I forgot about the door latch being hot. I burned myself throwing in some wood and used my finger to push the door closed." Seeing her roll her eyes at his stupidity he shrugged.

Waving him closer she held out her hand and snapped her fingers. Seeing the angry red marks across the back of his hand, she tsked and shook her head. "I swear you can't let a man do women's work." Dropping his hand she patted the couch beside her and made room for him. "You'll live tough guy. Just remember that they did invent those things called hot pads used specifically for hot things." Laughing she pointed to the one he was carrying in his other hand. "That's a hot pad Cole." He looked sheepishly at his uninjured hand and chuckled softly. "I used it after I burned my hand."

She threw herself back laughing harder unable to control it. "You are a piece of work Sun Wolf, you know that?"

Giving her a wolfish grin, he nodded his head. "Yeah, I'm one of a kind." Ruffling her hair, he laughed at her flushed face. He still saw shadows under her eyes and he felt a little sorry for her. Sobering, he pushed the emptied tray to the other end of the table and sat down. "Are you okay Becca?"

She wiped a tear from her cheek and nodded slowly. "I'm fine, just tired all of a sudden." Hiding her yawn behind a fist, she shrugged a shoulder. "I don't know why but I could use a nap." She felt his hand caress her hair and sighed.

"Hey, before you nod off sleepy head, I should tell you that I'm going to jump on my bike and try to head into town. I can make it easier knowing you are here safe. Do you mind?" Seeing a shadow cross her face, he reassured her. "I'll be fine trust me."

"I guess it's a good idea." Sitting up, she shrugged as she tried to hide the feeling of being excluded from the trip by looking away. "Would you stop by my place and get a few things? I'll write a quick note and you can explain to Grandda why I'm stuck here." Looking back at him, she wrinkled her nose at his groan and laughed. "Just tell him what he needs to know and get my stuff."

"Well let's get that note wrote so I can leave, the sooner I'm gone the sooner I'm back." Resting a hand on her shoulder for a moment, he dropped a light kiss on her cute little nose. "You just lay back and rest while I'm gone, okay?"

Smiling she nodded at him and snuggled down into the couch. "I promise."

When she heard him leave, she slowly hobbled to the bathroom despite her promising to stay put and groaned at her reflection in the mirror. Bruises and scratches covered her face, her eyes showed some swelling and the dark circles were ugly making her look like she had went three rounds with another boxer. Finding a brush in the vanity, she sat down gingerly and began working on her hair.

She stared down at the small braid and realized that she no longer needed to carry the reminder of her brother anymore. She had worn it beyond what the custom called for of one year. She had used it and the mourning of her dear brother to shut out the world and herself from the world in return.

Opening the drawer she had found the brush in, she dug around until she pulled out a pair of small scissors and quickly cut it off close to her scalp. "You were my hero when I was young, my friend when I got older and now you are my guardian, I love you Clint." Tying the cut end, she tucked it into her pocket and returned the scissors feeling as if a great weight had fallen from her shoulders.

After an hour of detangling, she felt her arms shaking with fatigue but pushed herself to finish. Making one long braid over her shoulder, she found a piece of string and secured the end. Letting her arms drop to her sides she sighed, now to get back to the couch without falling on my face, she thought.

She plotted her course carefully, leaning on the scattered furniture for support until she collapsed on her makeshift bed, exhausted. As she tried to get comfortable, she hoped Cole made it to town safe. The wind and rain still rattled at the windows but the thunder and lightening had lessened overnight. He had to fight the wind at his back on the way down into town and then again facing it on the way back. From what she could see of the weather through the window, he wouldn't be able to see more then a few feet in front of him.

Wiggling around she felt something poke her sharply in the hip and sat up. Digging between the cushions, her fingers found a hard shape, realized it was a book and pulled it out. Opening it she saw that is was a journal of sorts written in Coles' slanted handwriting and the beginning date was the day after Clint's death.

Unable to return it to its hiding place she slowly began to read, curious to see what he had written. She hadn't realized that he had gone through a far worse hell than she had for four years, believing he was unworthy to walk the earth. She read about his short lived but dangerous bout with booze and how one terrible dream had scared the daylights out of him, sobering him up after a week of steady drinking. He had wrote of his many jobs, none lasting more then a few weeks, earning him just enough to move on again. He mostly wrote about what was happening to him but not of how he felt. It was almost as if he wanted to keep a record of his movements not his emotions.

Closing the book, she shuddered to think that at one point he had almost given up on him self, until he found a man who reminded him so much of Clint. That man took Cole in, cleaned him up, gave him a good job and let him talk when he chose to, that is. It wasn't long before Cole realized he had something worth living for and it wasn't going to be found anywhere but back at home.

Swallowing past the lump in her throat, she wiped a tear away and held the book tightly to her chest. She felt anguish for him and anger towards herself for being so self centered. She wasn't the only one affected by Clint's death, they both had. Hell, the whole community had suffered in one way or another but she had been so blind to have seen it until now.

Tucking the book back where she had found it she laid back and closed her eyes. Now she knew more of the truth and it made her more determined to learn the rest of it, from his letters.

She did not know what time it was when he woke her but she knew it was dark. The fireplace and a few well-positioned lanterns gave the room a soft glow, telling her he had been back for a while. He was sitting on the back of the couch watching her with a soft look on his face.

"Hey, you're looking a little better."

Smiling, she slowly stretched and noticed she wasn't quite as stiff as she had been earlier. "Umm, feel better too." Reaching out she ran a hand up and down his arm. "How was your trip?"

Shrugging his shoulder, he scrubbed at his face. "The town's a mess as you can imagine. Trees and power lines are down everywhere along with the main phone lines. It's going to take some time to put everything to rights once the rain stops." Rubbing his temple, he sighed. "Three houses were hit by either trees or lightening and one is beyond repair. Everyone is accounted for though a few will be in the clinic with broken bones and assorted injuries."

She saw how this was affecting him and squeezed his arm. "Everyone made it through the worse of the storm and it'll be all right." Shifting to a more comfortable position, she looked around the room. "Did you get some of my things?" She really wanted those letters and some of her own clothing would be nice too.

"You're right. I'm just worrying about how we're going to get everything done before First Moon." Reaching down he pulled a stuffed bag to his lap. "Your mom packed everything you asked for and some extras. She said for you to stay put until the roads are clear and the rain stops. Which, by the way, it still hasn't slowed down." He laid the bag on her lap careful of her knees. "I had to tie it to my back so I could maneuver the bike. I had to hike the last two miles on foot when the bike bogged down in the mud." Seeing her facial expression, he laughed. "I doubt anyone would find it much less touch it if they did."

"I hope you're right." Sounding doubtful, she began digging in the bag for some real clothes. "I would hate to see that bike get stolen or wrecked."

"If they are stupid enough to try to get up this far and take it, more power to them. On top of everything else, there's been a small mud slide which is why I had to walk the last two miles."

"Oh hell, this isn't a good sign." Seeing the mud on the floor, she shook her head. "How long will it take to clean it all up?"

"A day or two, at the most. It depends on how many people can help with the clean up. I talked to Kyle and he said he would try to round up some guys and get up here as soon as the rain lets up." Helping her off the couch, he guided her to the bathroom so she could change. "I've been telling the council that it would happen and this storm had just enough moisture to make it happen. Luckily, it's a small slide."

They spent the remainder of the day and night quietly, both lost in their own thoughts until they shared their dinner before the fireplace where Cole made a comfortable nest for her. "I was wondering, well actually really curious why you were upset when you came out of the woods. Your wolf looked like it wanted to tear something apart."

Rebecca started talking about her time alone in the meadow before Cole had showed up and remembered the time after the change. The smell of the sun kissed grass, the first wildflowers blooming and the trees beginning to show their leaves as she ran around finally free. Describing the experience, she waved her spoon around wildly until she remembered that faint trail scent and dropped the utensil into the bowl as everything flooded back, making Cole jump at the sudden noise of her bowl breaking on the floor.

"Cole, I remember something else. When I was up there I found a faint scent that didn't belong in the meadow." Turning to face him she continued in a rush. "I followed it to the tree line then into the woods. I found some freshly turned earth and when I dug one up I found a trash bag full of pot."

His head snapped up when she said pot and he grabbed her hands roughly. "Are you sure Becca? It wasn't someone's trash?"

She shook her head and winced at the rough tone of his voice and grip of his hands. "Oh, it was defiantly pot, trust me. I know the smell too well. My neighbors, I should say my old neighbors used it a lot before they finally got arrested for selling."

Chapter 6

"Can you remember exactly where you found it Becca?" Jumping to his feet, he went in search for a pencil and notebook. "Can you make me a map?"

Nodding quickly she took the pencil and pad from him and began sketching a map of the meadow and trees. Explaining as she drew the spot she dug up she made xs where she had smelt out more of the cache. Finishing she looked up to see his face tight with controlled anger as he clinched and unclenched his fist. "Cole, what is it?"

"Remember when I told the council that we were having a problem with drugs lately? Well, we've actually been having a major trend." Rubbing the heels of his hands into his eyes, he sighed. "We've been having a problem with kids getting stoned lately and some of them have been caught with harder stuff. We cannot find out who is supplying or dealing because the kids will not talk. And if this stash is as big as you think, we may have someone here that's either growing it or making it some where on our land." He stared at the fire and growled. "We have to wait until it clears up before we can go up and we won't be able to pick up the scent then. The rain will have washed it away." Letting his frustration out on a piece of wood as he crushed it before throwing it in to the fire, he admitted they were running out of time and luck. "I need to talk to Rick."

Becca laid a hand on his tense arm. "We can't go any where now Cole, it's going to have to wait, only a fool would even try. I don't think that stuff is going anywhere any time soon, not in this weather." Feeling the tense muscles tighten even more she waited for him to explode but he closed his eyes and slowly relaxed.

"I hate to admit it but you are right. I just don't like knowing it's out there, waiting to be claimed and sold to our kids." He tossed another log into the fire sending sparks up the chimney. "I'm afraid we'll either find more then pot or we'll get there too late."

Lying back on his elbows, he let his head hang back easing tense muscles. "Then again, we may get exceptionally lucky and beat whoever is behind this up there." Grinning he wiggled his foot impatiently. "I would love to be hanging around to see whose stuff that is and bust their slimy ass."

Rebecca could not help but laugh at his frustration and his veiled threat. Pushing herself up and on the couch, she sat behind him and tried to pull him into a sitting position. "You just want to kick someone's ass, admit it." Patting the front of the couch between her legs, she got his attention. As he settled between her knees, she slowly began kneading his shoulders. "Not that I wouldn't love to see it happen and help out." Working her fingers into the muscles she slowly felt them relax and his shoulders droop just a little. "I would like to get some answers to those dreams of mine."

"Damn right I do! That poison can't be permitted to be around here. It messes up our kids, who already have enough problems these days. The people who bring it in, grow it or sell it are just sick." Ticking off the things that make him angry on his fingers, he brought up his head. "We've got enough problems with petty theft, vandalism, runaway's and fights with our teens and adding that crap only makes it a hundred times worse."

Waving a hand before his face, she waited until she got his attention. "Hey, we all know the arguments and the majority of our people would agree with you. But just remember we've been lucky enough to find out about the stuff and we can stop it." Yawning loudly behind her hand she shook her head to get rid of the fuzzy feeling growing in her head. "I'm just glad I remembered it."

Cole laid his head back and took a close look at Becca realizing she was beginning to show serious signs of being tired. "Hey, let's get you to bed. You look like you're ready to keel over." Tugging a stray strand of her hair behind her ear, he saw her eyes grow heavier. "It's late and we both could use some serious sleep."

Nodding she watched the flames as they danced hypnotically in front of her as her fingers played with his hair. She felt herself begin to sway with the flames but shook herself out of it. "If you don't mind I would rather sleep down here tonight. I really don't want to have to climb those stairs." Peaking at him from under her lashes, she hoped he would understand.

Cole caught the nervous flutter of her hands on his shoulder and did understand. "I'll bring down some pillows and another blanket. The couch is pretty comfortable so you'll be comfortable. I'll just kick back in the chair and keep you company, so I don't mind." He pulled her head down to look at her drooping eyes. "I don't expect anything from you Becca and if your company is all you're ready to give, that's fine."

Smiling weakly she nodded and let out the breath she had been holding. "Thank you Cole, for everything."

Once she was settled on the couch, Cole moved around the house quietly, cleaning up their dishes and laying wood in the stove for the morning. Hearing the wind losing some of its ferocity he hoped it would all blow over by morning. When he checked on her later she was sleeping peacefully, curled under the blanket with her hand under her cheek.

He added more wood to the fireplace and sat in the easy chair beside the couch, watching her. Laying his head on his fist, he watched her smile tenderly as she dreamt and reached out to her, caressing her hair. When she frowned, he gently rubbed his thumb over the furrows in her brow until they disappeared. Letting his eyes drift closed and letting his hand slid back to her hair, he felt at peace with himself for the first time in years.

When she tossed her head under his hand he sat up quickly and whispered to her that it was okay, she was safe now. As she calmed she turned her head into his hand and sighed deeply.

"Cole," she whispered softly as she snuggled in her blanket.

Rebecca woke slowly when the quietness and stillness slowly invaded her dreams. She sat up listening, only hearing the fire crackling and Cole's soft breathing. The wind had died away to a soft breeze and the rain had finally stopped some time after she had fallen asleep. She watched Cole as he slept, his face easy and his arm hanging over the side of the chair. For the first time since she had seen him a few days ago he looked completely relaxed.

He really hadn't aged much in almost five years unlike she had thought, though he did have more sun creases around his eyes now. He had filled out more too. His chest and shoulders were broader and more developed almost as if he had done a lot of physical labor in the last four years.

His hair was much longer then she remembered, just past his shoulder blades now but it looked good on him, kind of sexy, even. Closing her eyes she saw him as he looked back then and decided she liked the more mature Cole.

Pulling her duffle bag around the end of the couch quietly she knew she had the perfect opportunity to read the letters he had sent. Sliding her arm into the bag, she dug around until she felt the stack with her searching fingers. She got a better grip and slowly wiggled them out of the bag and laid them on her lap. Sliding the bag back, she checked to see if she had disturbed him. Seeing him shift his shoulders to a more comfortable position, she smiled softly.

Untying the leather string, she took the first letter and stared at the envelope, dated four weeks after Clint's funeral and from Washington. Carefully opening the envelope she realized she did not feel any of her old bitter emotions well up inside.

She tried to read but there was not enough light so she gathered the letters and her blanket up and slowly hobbled closer to the fire for better light. When she was finally seated before the fire and comfortable, she began reading. When finished, she laid each one on the floor beside her. She learned so much about Cole through those pieces of paper, more then she had learned from his journal.

He had poured his heart out, ranting about the injustice of life and his fellow human beings. He had found beautiful words to describe the beauty of the world and he even showed he had the soul of a poet when he described the sunset in the Everglades of Florida.

She read of his love and deep respect for Clint, the regret of not being there with him and his shame. He had apologized repeatedly for leaving and he pleaded with her to forgive him. She read between the lines and saw that he had loved her through the years and he still did according to his last letter.

She cried with each letter as she realized she had been so blind and stupid, her pride had been so strong that she had closed out the world along with him. Now that the door had finally been opened, it exposed a bright and wonderful place, new to her.

Laying the last letter on the pile she turned and saw Cole in a new light, he was a man who had made mistakes but owned up to them. He was hard but gentle and he was the only one who had ever touched her heart. She loved his earthy poetry, honest and telling. It touched not only her heart but also her soul. She felt renewed by his words, she felt her heart fill with hope, and she felt her spirit's jubilation over being included in all his letters.

She had always thought she had been a whole person but now she realized that she had been less then half of everything. She had been only half alive, half living, and half empty in her heart and soul, barely existing. She had become as a spirit in this world, never there, touching no one or nothing. The last four years had been meaningless, a waste of precious time and she was unable to make them up.

She lay down on the thick rug, pulling the letters to her chest and just stared at the sleeping man in his chair. She watched him until her eyes grew heavy, smiling as she drifted into another peaceful sleep.

Cole watched her through cracked eyelids until she fell asleep, careful to keep himself relaxed. He had been watching her for some time as she poured over those old letters. Seeing her cry, laugh, frown, smile and sigh repeatedly he knew she had finally and truly saw him for what he was. He had poured everything he had been and still was into those letters trying to reach her as he bared his soul.

When she finished he saw her eyes glitter and her face glowed as she went deep into her own thoughts. He knew she had come to some important decisions and realizations. He saw the old Becca coming out finally. He sighed as she mumbled his name in her sleep and hoped things were going to turn around for them and the future.

Becca woke the next morning to find herself back on the couch and hearing Coles cheerful whistling through the open back door. Sitting up she looked for the letters she had fell asleep holding and felt panicked when she didn't find them. She really didn't want him to know she had them much less that she had spent hours finally reading them late last night.

She stood slowly, testing her knees and sighed when they were only tender today and didn't threaten to give out on her. Padding barefoot to the door, she watched him as he set up another piece of wood to be split in two from the pile behind him.

She watched his arm muscles bulge against the sleeve of his shirt as he swung the ax over his head and split the wood cleanly. It was fascinating to see the muscles bulge, tighten and ripple with each movement. She remembered the feeling of those movements under her hands, around her body and felt a blush creep up her face.

When she saw him peel off his t-shirt she must have moaned because his head shot up surprised he had an audience. She blushed harder when he gave her his slow sexy smile winking and looked away quickly as he bent to pick up another piece of wood. He was torturing her with every deliberate move he made and she needed to keep herself under control.

"Morning," He repeated, watching her face as it flushed more and more. "How'd you sleep?"

Watching his eyes as they squinted up against the morning sun, she caught her breath. "Um, good, thanks,' she stammered embarrassed he had caught her practically drooling. "You moved me to the couch." Duh, she thought pinching herself. "Um, what did you do with the letters?" She looked at the high mountainside avoiding his knowing eyes. She was embarrassed but didn't know why since he had sent them and he knew what he wrote.

"I put them back in your bag." He caught her fidgeting and decided they needed to get it out in the open, now. "I didn't know you'd kept them."

Her head snapped up and her eyes went wide. "I never intended to but something always kept me from getting rid of them." Shrugging she stepped out and turned to the east. The suns rays caressed her like an old friend. "When they arrived either my mother or I would just put them in a stack and I would hide them in a drawer. Back then I didn't want to know what you said but since I've come back everything's changed." Hearing him cross the distance to the steps, she looked down at him seeing his encouragement to go on. "Last night was the first time I've read them."

"And,' he kept his voice soft as he smiled softly. "what else?"

She wrapped her arms around the rail post, laying her head against it. "And I think I know you better now then ever before. You've changed from a careless, wild young person to a very responsible, mature beyond his years, caring man."

He took a step up, keeping to the other side of the steps and watched her closely. "And?"

She smiled as she turned, standing against the post, hands in her pockets. "You're a poet at heart. You see the world as it really is, good, bad, beautiful and ugly. You've tried to make a difference, make it better."

He took another slow step up towards her and gave her time to go on. "And?"

She leaned her head against the post and swallowed back the sudden tears. "You regret many things Cole and at one time in your letters you listed them all like they were what made you ugly. But they didn't really, they made you change, grow and become a better man."

She wiped away a tear and barked a laugh. "You used your regrets to improve where I used mine to hide from the world." Closing her eyes, she took a deep breath and struggled to go on. "I held on to my grief, used it as a shield. That shield turned into a wall that kept everything in and out, depending on how it affected me. I locked the old memories in a room and turned my back to it. I didn't want to remember the good things. I just clung to the bad. I let the bad emotions and memories feed me the poison until I was no longer Becca."

He reached the last step and wanted to hold her but held back. She needed to get it all out and he wouldn't interfere. "And?' he whispered encouraging her to continue.

"You told me in so many ways that you loved me. Every letter, every thought, every word was filled with your love. And I was a fool to ignore it, to hide it and to hide from what could have been."

He stepped to the porch, leaned against the opposite post folding his arms, and waited.

"I buried myself in the anger, bitterness and blame towards you until I forgot that there had been us and the love we shared. I wrapped the wrong feelings around me until I shut myself off from the world and myself. I used those emotions to the point were I became empty except of the anger." Shaking her head, she laughed sadly. "Until I came home and found out that I had left my heart here and I was so wrong in doing it." Looking at him, she stood straighter. "I was wrong to try to bury the love Cole. And if you can find it in you to forgive me, it's still here if you want it."

Seeing him stand straighter, she stepped back and searched his face. She didn't hide anything from him, it was all there, the fear of being too late, the love that drove her and the need to have him in her life.

Feeling his breath caressing her face as he stood toe to toe with her, his hands sliding along her jaw, she tipped her head and caught her breath. His face was so close, so alight and so beautiful to her at that moment.

"Do you know how long I've waited for you to say that you love me?" Taking a ragged breath, he closed his eyes. "I held on day after day, year after year, hoping against hope that you'd find the love deep inside your heart." He crushed her against him and held her tightly. "I never gave up hope Becca because I couldn't. I need you to complete me and make me whole."

She sobbed quietly clinging to him knowing she had almost lost him. She had finally fought the right fight for once in her life, the fight to keep her mate. "I love you Cole, I always have and always will."

He pulled away just enough to see the love shining from deep with in her and felt his soul fill with that light. He slowly kissed her letting her feel his love filling her soul with it.

She drank in his gently kiss, letting it fill her to over flowing and it was the softness of his telling lips that was her undoing.

His hands slid under her shirt, roaming her back, feeling her heated skin. She felt the muscles lose the tension and she melted into him as his hands slowly slid across her ribs to cup her breasts. She broke the kiss as a moan from deep inside her escaped her lips. She didn't care if they were standing outside, she only cared that he kept touching her.

He watched the hunger in her eyes grow when he gently ran his thumbs across her bra and the hardened nubs underneath.

She arched her back, silently demanding more. She felt as if she was on fire and he was the only one who could douse the flames. When his hands slowly slid back to her ribs she whimpered, trying to hold him where he was. She felt him slide down her body and rested his head on her stomach making her gasp.

When he slid her shirt up, she shivered as the air blew across her hot skin and when his face slid across her sensitive skin, he made her stomach muscles tighten. She found herself gasping as he gently placed light kisses on her constricting muscles.

As he slowly kissed his way along her ribs, she wound her fingers through his hair, feeling its silky length brush her skin with his movements. As he reached the bottom of her bra cup, she began panting and tossed her head back closing her eyes.

He lightly ran his tongue along the small cup line below her breast knowing he was driving her crazy but continued her torment. He had to find out just how far she would let him go before she cracked. When he moved to her other breast she tightened her grip in his hair, trying to pull him up a little higher but he wouldn't budge.

They didn't hear the knock at the front door or it opening right after another knock. They were so wrapped up in each other that they only heard each other's breathing.

"Any one home," Max Red Wolf called through the house as he entered. "Cole? Becca, are you here?"

Becca froze and pulled Cole from her by his hair. "Grandda's here!" She hissed gasping for breath. "Cole, Grandda's here!"

Cole groaned as her words slowly sank in to his hazy mind and she began pushing him away. He swore as he helped her straighten her clothes and tried to shield her from her approaching grandfather. He saw her take a deep calming breath and knew it was going to be obvious no matter what they did to hide it from the old man.

She turned, patting her hair and plastering a smile on her flushed face. "We're back here." She waved frantically to Cole to go back to his wood chopping as she called into the house. Taking several more deep breaths she hoped she appeared somewhat normal to her grandfather as he came through the door.

She knew she had failed miserably the instant he gave her a knowing look and laughed. She blushed profusely and hid her face in her hands. So much for acting like nothing happened.

"I can see you're feeling better." He grumbled at her hidden face. "I take it you're happy though."

She refused to look at him but nodded sharply. She listened to him cross the porch in one stride and slowly descended the steps. Peeking through her spread fingers, she watched Cole hold out his hand to her grandfather in welcome. She saw him stand proudly before Grandfather, not even flinching under the Elders intimidating and searching stares.

As they began talking, she relaxed a little knowing her grandfather would save his questions about their relationship until later. She only hoped it would be later before he broached the subject, much later.

She slowly went down to join them, to stand beside her grandfather and wrapped an arm around his hips. "Hi Grandda." Looking up she let him give her a quick peck on her heated cheek.

"Hi pumpkin. I see you guys survived the storm well enough." He took her chin and examined her face. He ignored her sparkling eyes but concentrated on the bruises and cuts. "You look like you got into one hell of a fight, kiddo. But what I want to know is who won?" He released her, shaking his head. "Cole told us what happened when he came by yesterday. Your mother is beside herself with worry, which is why I'm here."

Cole nodded in understanding and then glanced to the side of the house. "How did you get here, sir? I know you're not foolish enough to have walked all the way here." Looking at the Elders feet, he grinned seeing they were bare, as usual and clean.

The old man chuckled and slapped the younger man on the shoulder. "I maybe old but I am not crazy. I rode my horse of course." He whistled shrilly and a whinny answered from the front of the house. "He's sure footed and we took our time but that's neither here or there."

Looking around he took in the view of this place and the two young people before him. He ignored the tension and the unmistaken scent of mating lingering in the air. Instead, he concentrated on the beauty of the mountain in front of him.

Becca fidgeted when she felt Cole raking his eyes over her while Max looked elsewhere. She couldn't hide the want she still felt burning inside her and she saw that he felt the same way. His eyes held the promise of picking up where they left off, but later.

Max cleared his throat loudly when he caught the pair sneaking hot looks at each other. "Okay, I came, I saw and I'm gone."

He stepped forward, shaking Coles hand again and sent him a quick look of acceptance. "About time if you ask me,' he grumbled for Cole's ears alone. "Do right by her and you'll never regret it,' he added before turning to his beloved granddaughter.

He hugged her close and felt her happiness and wellbeing vibrating through her. Kissing the top of her head, he poured all his love in to it. "I love you pumpkin." He said the rest silently and he knew she heard him loud and clear.

She snuggled closer and whispered, "Love you too Grandda." She knew he wasn't shocked or upset about the way her life had suddenly changed course. He accepted her choices and she felt his joy in them. "And thank you."

She felt the rumble in his chest before he released her, his eyes sparkled and his only answer was a cheeky wink.

Watching him leave, waving over his shoulder she shook her head before turning to Cole. The smoldering look in his eyes stole the breath from her lungs. Feeling herself slowly stepping closer, letting his eyes draw her in and she could read his thoughts. She silently told him she was ready and wanting his touch more then ever.

However, another un-welcomed visitor again interrupted them when they heard a four wheeler coming around the house. Cole swore at his growing annoyance and stepped back from Becca's leaning body. "This had better be damn important or I swear I'm going to hurt him." He growled as he stalked past her pausing long enough to drop a hard kiss on her quivering lips. "I'll be back."

She stood there, fingers on her tender lips and gulped in air to her starving lungs. Even that quick kiss had made her body shake with want and need. She slowly climbed the steps and went inside, closing the door quietly behind her.

She heard two male voices through the open windows and kept to the back of the house. She recognized Kyle's voice right away. It was a little deeper then his younger brothers but had the same rich timber. She loved Kyle but only as another brother and she quickly remembered that he always treated her as if she was a nuisance.

She didn't want anyone or everyone in the community to know that she was here and had been for two nights. She refused to be the newest fuel for the gossips fire and she sure didn't want Cole to be another point of their talk, again.

She busied herself in the kitchen, becoming familiar with the cupboards and the now running fridge. Opening the pantry, she saw that everything was in a jumbled up mess, no organization what so ever. Shaking her head, she began to methodically clean and reorganize the shelves just to keep her busy. As she wiped the dust off of the bottom shelf, she noticed the shelf liner wasn't glued down but laid into place unlike the others. Pulling it out, she saw a thick envelope flutter to the floor at her feet.

Picking it up, she saw it was addressed to Cole, dated just over six months ago in a shaky but slanted bold writing. She was curious as to why an old letter was hiding in the kitchen pantry and how it got there in the first place. Putting it on the counter she finished her chore and cleaned her rag out with soap and water.

She still heard the men talking and wished Kyle would leave already as she paced the now spotless kitchen. When she heard chainsaws running she knew it was going to be quite some time before the coast was clear for her to move around freely. She began pacing, feeling like a prisoner in a cell and then got an idea. Seeing that no one needed to clear the back of the house, she could go out there, in the open fresh air. She tiptoed to the back door and quietly let herself out.

She stopped half way to the back fence and remembered that she really should leave some kind of note for Cole but didn't want to go back into the house. Smiling mischievously, she spied the kindling pile.

Arranging some pieces in the middle of the cleared walkway, she dusted her hands off and nodded in satisfaction. Arrows and a pair of wings should let him know what she was doing and where she was going. Ducking behind the woodshed she quickly shucked off her clothes and stretched, feeling free as she called forth her eagle spirit.

She slowly changed feeling no struggle or pain this time. Taking off from the ground, beating her wings with powerful strokes she became airborne easily. As she climbed higher, she cried out with the pure joy of being in the air again and began doing an aerial dance. Her dipping and diving turned into slow circles or wing tip turns until she just began flying towards the meadow.

Spying a perfectly shaded limb on an old pine she landed a little awkwardly, her leg joints still a little sore. Settling her wings, she looked over her meadow, seeing no damage to speak of from the storm. Looking at the ground, several yards below her she saw one of the spots she had found earlier now looking like a small mud puddle. Gliding to the tree line, she saw the bag that she had dug up earlier, still laying beside it. She cocked her head at it catching the faint smell of the drug and knew she had to get someone up here soon.

There was no telling how long the bag would go unnoticed or reclaimed but the longer it was out in the open the more likely it would be claimed. She knew if she put out a call others would hear and come but she did not trust everyone. She had to get some of the bags contents, rebury it and get the evidence back to Cole before time and her luck ran out.

Once she figured all that out she realized she would have to do multiple changes into her human form then to her wolf form and back to her eagle. She just hoped she was up for it, she had never attempted this many changes in a short time. Making sure that there was no way she was going to be interrupted, she slowly began to change. Working quickly she opened the bag and pulled out a small baggie and re-closed the trash bag just as she had found it.

Rolling the bag into the dirty water laying in the hole, making it overflow, she hoped the bags would leak and ruin the contents, making them worthless. She pushed the bag down as far as she could, before pulling mud, pine needles and old leaves over it. She slowly stood and checked her surroundings again. Picking up a fallen limb, she smoothed the ground over and around the hole. She worked until she hid any evidence that the cache had been discovered or it had been tampered with.

She decided that her wolf wouldn't be needed so she changed back to her eagle and silently apologized to her wolf for not letting it help or out for a while. Wrapping her talons around the small bag, she took off silently, promising the wolf it would be free as soon as possible.

She flew quickly, keeping as high as she could, hoping no one could see that she was carrying something and she was in a hurry. Everyone knew when another shape shifter was in spirit form, the shifter was larger than its natural counterparts were and they had the ability to speak as a human or their spirit animal.

As she glided over the valley, she saw that few of the population paid attention or noticed her. They were busy trying to get the storm damage cleaned up. She caught an up draft until she was above Cole's house and gently banked to the right. Landing close to where she had taken off, she changed then walked towards the shed seeing him sitting on the back porch nursing a beer.

She calmly dressed keeping the baggie under her foot when she could even though she was a bundle of nerves. Brushing off some of the caked mud on her feet and legs, she finally gave up as it clung to her stubbornly. As she crossed the yard, she was careful of the wood splinters under her bare feet.

Reaching the steps and smiling smugly up to him, she suddenly felt proud of herself. "I've got something for you."

Seeing his slow smile, she laughed and shook her head. "It is not what you are thinking, you silly man." She had hid the purloined evidence behind her back as she had approached the house. She couldn't help it if she was very proud of her self and her successful mission. Climbing the steps, she slowly brought her hand forward from behind her back, holding the bag in her pinched fingers fearing the smell would contaminate her somehow.

When he saw her present, he slowly set his beer bottle down on the low table with a shaky hand and eyed it carefully.

She dropped it in his open hand and wiped her fingers on her shorts before pulling a face. "And there's a lot more up there, for now anyway."

"I should have known you'd find a way to get up there." Chuckling he shook his head in amazement at her ingenuity.

"You are fantastic Lady and crazy at the same time." Pulling her onto his lap, he hugged her tightly. "Just don't do that again."

She leaned back and flinched when she saw mild anger flashing in his eyes. She tried to explain herself but he put his hand over her mouth to stop her.

"I'm proud of you for going but you've taken one hell of a chance." He glared at her until she nodded. "So tell me, what brought all of this on?"

She quietly told him everything as he held the bag, examining it closely. When she finished her story, he slipped the bag into his shirt pocket.

"Well, you at least thought it out and I would say you covered your tracks well enough." He hugged her again before sliding her off his legs. "While you were out playing Nancy Drew we cleared the driveway, the road and the power is back on. But unfortunately the phones are still dead." Tucking her under his arm, he led her into the house. "We need to call Rick and get him up here."

She stopped and frowned confused. "But if the phones are down, how are you going to call him?"

He grinned and pointed at the hand radio lying on the counter "Radio, my dear. Every Guardian and Border Watch has one. Channel one is for us, two is for the clinic." He picked it up and keyed it. As he spoke to Rick, she motioned him not to mention her or the drugs outright. When he nodded in understanding, she fanned herself in relief.

When Rick said he would stop by in an hour, she looked at herself and back at Cole in horror. She pointed up and headed for the shower to get herself presentable.

As she stood under the hot spray, she found herself giggling. She hadn't done anything that spontaneous or covert since she tried sneaking out of the house at sixteen but then Grandda had caught her.

She finished her shower and almost jumped out of her skin when Cole slid the shower door open unexpectedly. She hadn't heard him come in to the bathroom over the sound of the running water. She instinctively covered herself but slowly dropped her arms when he gave a low whistle. "Towel please." She repeated it when he leaned his elbow on the towel rack.

"Hmmm,' he ran his eyes up her wet body slowly. "The bruises are fading nicely." He ducked when she took a halfhearted swing at him.

"Cole, towel please." She tried to grab the towel but he moved closer putting his body between her and the towel rack. She folded her arms and stared back at him in annoyance. "We can stand here forever but I don't think Rick would be thrilled to make a wasted trip."

Cole bowed and stepped back a pace, hating to admit she was right. He thought about calling Rick and postponing the meeting but he knew work before pleasure was the rule. "You can bet I will finish what we started earlier. That's a promise Becca." He wiggled an eyebrow and left her to get presentable. "Oh, I brought up your bag, it's on the bed."

She stuttered a soft thanks as she wrapped the large towel around her feeling her blush creep up her neck. Grabbing another towel, she hid behind it as she worked on her hair. When she heard his chuckle, she turned her head and stuck out her tongue at him before he left.

Chapter 7

When she was ready to get dressed, she found him standing outside the door and caught her breath. She saw his eyes go smoky, filled with yearning and she felt her body respond in kind. Gripping the towel tightly around her, she shook her head slowly. Even as she denied him knowing they were about to have company, her body screamed yes. She watched his slow smile grow and knew he was planning to finish what he had started, as soon as possible.

Taking a deep breath, she approached him and laid a hand on his chest. "I have to get dressed Cole."

He felt her cool hand on him and clinched a hand behind his back. He kept a tight grip on himself and let her pass.

She grinned to herself and quickly walked to his room, dropping her towel at the door. Closing the door with a soft click behind her, she giggled when she heard his loud moan. She did not know why she had put fuel on the fire but she defiantly enjoyed it.

Dressing in a pair of light cotton shorts and matching tank top she looked at all the bruises covering her body. They were now more pronounced in color, in size but not as painful. She leaned towards the mirror to get a closer look at her face and decided the scraps were not all that bad today. In addition, the dark circles had completely faded while her almond shaped eyes glittered and glowed.

Combing her wet hair, she thought of getting it cut to a more manageable length but quickly decided against it. Gathering it in a loose ponytail, she secured it, letting it hang free so that it would dry faster. Beside long hair had proven to quite interesting lately, something she wouldn't mind exploring again with Cole.

As she left the room, she heard him singing in the shower and resisted the urge to barge in like he almost did with her. Keeping her hand pressed gently on the door, she felt a wave of desire wash through her again. Before she acted on that desire, she stepped away, remembering his promise. Blinking away the memory of their lovemaking in the meadow, she quietly went down stairs.

Cole knew she was standing outside and was surprised that he could feel her there debating to come in or not. He had kept singing and felt her when she finally left, shortly after the chorus line of the Gambler, grinning as the image of her retreating back and the towel falling flashed through his mind. He had to admit that he was a little shocked and surprised at her brazen move. If she had known how close he had been to taking her right here in the bathroom, she wouldn't have done it.

It took all of his control not to touch her much less say what he wanted. However, she was right, the time was not right and he prayed he could hold back on to his urges until things were right. Finishing his shower, he quickly dried forcing his mind to concentrate on the drug find and Rick's' pending visit.

Cole quickly closed the door behind Rick and felt elation over the fact that by this time tomorrow they would have the drugs under wraps. His frustration was over the fact that they couldn't seize the person at the same time slowly died, knowing they were about to put a serious hurt on the drug ring was enough for now. In addition, he had to admit that he had a lot of pride in Becca for giving Rick a very detailed description of where she found the goods and how she found them.

Hell, Rick got enough information that he didn't have a single question for her except when he was getting ready to leave. In addition, Cole wanted to kick himself in the rear for not thinking of it himself.

What had Becca done to cover her scents during today's excursion? Her answer had been an unnerving, nothing.

She hadn't thought of it save brushing over the dirt and her tracks with a tree limb. She looked up at him and stopped mid step. "I really messed up, didn't I?"

He could feel her anger mixed with fear build inside her until she began trembling. He couldn't help but feel his own build as the possible repercussions flashed through his mind. The fear of her being found out and a possible reprisal made him determined to protect her at all costs, even with his own life.

Schooling his face to appear calm, he quickly reassured her as he rubbed the back of his neck. "Hey, we don't know that whoever is behind this will know it was you. Besides, you can't go home now." He stepped around the couch and pulled her stiff body against him. "I'll keep you safe until this is over, I promise."

Leaning into him, she let his body warm her chilled skin and nodded. "I know you will but what about my family, Cole? Could they possibly be in danger now?"

Cole let the realization sink in that she was right and groaned. He let her go and raced for the radio, calling Rick to hightail it back, immediately. He had let her down with her brother and he was not going to let it happen again. "We'll protect them Becca, nothing is going to happen, I swear."

Nodding she swallowed nervously past the lump in her throat. "I know you will Cole, you're a protector." Slipping under his arm, she gave him a soft smile. "And you don't tell lies."

When Rick pounded on the door a minute later they joined him outside to voice their concern. As Cole explained Becca's fears, he held her close to him, making it obvious where she belonged.

Rick took it as inevitable and did not comment on the possessive way Cole held Becca. He saw the way they had been watching each other earlier and he was willing to bet they had either already claimed each other or were about to very soon. In addition, he liked what she had done to Cole's confidence. He was more alive now, then he had been in the last six months and that was a good sign.

A man like Cole needed a strong, good-natured woman to give him balance. However, he was a little surprised that this little bit of a woman had the power to tame the big bad wolf.

After Rick reassured them repeatedly that Rebecca's family would not be unprotected or harmed, he took his leave for the second time. He caught a faint scent on the air but dismissed it as nothing. He didn't hear anything but a few birds and the breeze in the pines, calling himself paranoid for letting the developing situation make him overly sensitive.

Cole led Becca into the house and closed the door behind them gently, shutting out the evening chill. He hung back as she looked over her shoulder, catching his look of worry. He silently vowed that no matter what happened he would protect her and her family, anyway he could. Wrapping his arms around her, he reassured her everything would be okay.

Nodding she leaned back into him and held his arms tightly. "I know you will."

"Okay, what's wrong now? You've been acting kind of funny for the last few hours and it's starting to get to me." Leaning he tried to look into her eyes. "Becca, what is it?"

"I found a letter in the pantry, addressed to you. I think it's from your father." Patting his arms, she stepped away and went to get it. "I think it was written just before he died." Grabbing the letter off the edge of the counter she went back to him and held it out to him. Seeing his large hand tremble as he took it and the look of mistrust on his face, she stepped back. "I'll leave you alone if you want me to."

"No, it's all right." Sitting on the couch, he tore the letter open and groaned. There were two letters inside, one still in a yellowed envelope. "I don't believe this." Whispering he handed the sealed letter to Becca, shaking his head. "He promised me that he would give this to you when I left."

Taking the letter, she looked at it then up to him. He had left a letter for her, just as he said. Only it had never been delivered to her. "I don't need to read this now Cole. Let sleeping dogs lie." Trying to hand it back to him, she smiled. "It doesn't matter anymore."

"It does to me Becca. Please, open it." Covering her hand with his he pushed it back to her before pulling her down to sit beside him. "Please."

"Okay Cole, if it's what you want." Tearing open the envelope, she took a deep breath as she slid the papers out. When something landed in her lap she looked down to see a simple solitaire diamond ring laying there. Gasping she looked up to him, searching his face. "Cole?"

"In the letter I asked you to wait for me because I would be back soon. I was going to give this to you that night but couldn't considering." Taking the ring, he held it up for her. "It's not an engagement ring, just a promise ring."

She wiped a tear from her cheek and smiled as she slipped her finger through the ring. "A promise you kept. You came back."

"But not soon enough," grumbling he swallowed his anger towards his father. It wouldn't do any good to harbor ill feelings against the dead.

"It does not matter anymore, Cole." Whispering she caressed his face. "A promise kept is a promise fulfilled."

"Are you going to read the letter?" Clearing his throat nervously he folded and unfolded the letter to him from his father.

"No. I know what it says and that's all that matters." Putting the letter into the envelope, she smiled up to him. "When we're old and gray, maybe I'll read it."

"Are we going to grow old and gray?" Brushing her hair back, he held his breath. "Becca?"

"I think you're going to look devastatingly handsome gray." Grinning she kissed his hand. "But for now, let's concentrate on the re-start of our lives."

As she lay awake, she gauged Coles sleep. He had worked hard to clear the storm damage with his brother and the closest neighbors and now he slept hard. She should be asleep herself but worrying about her family had chased the sleep away. She carefully eased her legs off the edge of the bed and felt him stir, holding her breath, she waited until he settled on his back. When she knew it was safe she slid off the bed and grabbed her nightshirt.

Quickly tiptoeing to the door, she paused once to make sure he still slept and slipped out of the room. Pacing the dark living room, she tried to convince herself that everything would work out in the end. They would get the drugs first thing in the morning and they would figure out who owned them. Nevertheless, she couldn't ignore the nagging feeling they were missing something. Something small had been overlooked and it was going to prove disastrous.

Feeling the unfamiliar weight of the small ring on her finger, she raised it to the moon light. She never would have thought he would get her a ring, but to learn he had intended to give it to her the night Clint had died, almost broke her heart. Moreover, for both of them to learn that his father was the one responsible for keeping them apart, hurt much worse.

He said he had never approved of their relationship, they were too young and he didn't feel right knowing his son was falling in love with the Shaman's granddaughter. Therefore, he lied to them both, hoping to save them from each other. He believed he was right in what he did until Cole made a rare visit home. He was devastated to know that Cole had been so close to losing himself, only then did he realize he had been wrong in his thinking.

His fear of finally telling the truth and admitting he was wrong, kept him from saying anything for another two years. When Cole finally came home to stay, the guilt had been too much. He wrote the letter, took Coles letter to her and hid them, hoping they'd be found before it was too late. His final wish was that they would find each other once again and they would find it in their hearts to some day forgive a stupid prideful old man.

Becca had held Cole when he finally read the letter aloud and saved her comments until he was done. When he had finished she watched him as he let a single tear roll down his face. Holding him tightly she rocked him as he stared at the letter lying on his lap and she shed the tears for both of them. He didn't say anything for a long time and when he finally did, he whispered, 'I forgive you'.

They didn't say much to each other after that, his simple words had been enough. She did notice that he would get a sad look in his eyes but it went away when he turned to her. She knew it would take time for him to accept it but he would, now that she was there to help him.

She felt Coles presence slowly approach her and she sighed as her worries faded a little. "I didn't want to wake you."

"Your absence woke me and your thinking,' he sighed as he touched her shoulder. "You think too loudly sometimes." Pulling her back against him, he wrapped his arms around her shoulders in a comforting hold.

"I couldn't sleep, I keep thinking of what might happen and it scares me." She held his arms and shuddered. "I wish I hadn't gone up there."

"Should a, could a, would a, Becca. Don't beat yourself up about it." Squeezing gently he pressed a light kiss to her hair. "You stumbled into an already existing problem, not caused it." Leaning to the side, he watched her smile a little. "Hell, you helped us when you found the stuff, saving us weeks or months of chasing our tails."

She giggled when he shook her gently. "I guess you're right."

"That's my girl. Now, come on, we need to get some sleep." He stressed the last word, telling her he was going to be a perfect gentleman tonight. "We have a very busy day tomorrow and we have a celebration to attend afterwards."

Becca stiffened as he brought up the ceremony and groaned as she hung her head. "I completely forgot about it." She made a rude noise, covered her mouth as she shook her head.

"Don't feel like you're the only one because I forgot too. Rick reminded me before he left." Shaking her gently he laughed. "We'll be fine, okay? We'll get the drugs and some rest to be ready to join the celebration, no problem. Unless we don't get any sleep at all tonight, that is."

She returned to his arms and chewed her lip in thought. "I think we had better get sleep tonight or I won't be able to dance or sing worth a darn."

"Hmm, sleep and performing or fun and weariness, tough choice." Chuckling he caught her hand as she pinched him on the ribs. Leading her back upstairs, he promised himself he would hold off another day, before claiming her as his. He fully intended on claiming her forever, even if it killed him.

The next day broke clear and warm, promising to be unusually hot for the time of year. As they packed a backpack with some essentials, they did little talking working side by side comfortably. Once they were ready, they headed out on his dirt bike to the rendezvous point agreed on earlier. Becca had to hold her legs over his knees because bending them for too long proved to be painful.

As they parked the bike close to the meadow, Becca heard several other small engine vehicles approach. She let out a held breath when Rick, the other Guardians and Kyle arrived on big ATV's. She waved at TJ and walked as fast as she could to her, seeing her wave back enthusiastically.

They quickly exchanged news of the last few days as if they were old friends. When Becca heard that Chris was showing signs of improvement, she hugged TJ. "I told you he would be okay!"

"He'll be able to attend the ceremony but won't be able to participate, doctors and my orders." TJ gave her a toothy grin and flashed her cat eyes. "I'll make sure of it."

Becca laughed as she helped the woman unload the shovels and the empty crate. "Well, lets get this over with before I jump out of my skin." Leading the way across the meadow, she sighed seeing that nothing seemed to have been disturbed since yesterday. As she approached the reburied cache, she pointed out several of the other spots to everyone.

When they split up into pairs, Rick informed her that she would have the job of look out while everyone else worked. Ducking behind a bush she quickly changed in to an eagle and took to the sky as fast as her wings would take her. She slowly circled until she found a good vantage point and landed well beyond where her companions quickly set to digging.

Before long, they had confiscated over seventeen bags full of not only pot but also what Rick claimed looked like uncut cocaine. Kyle took a bag and took an experimental taste of the white powder, then spit it out. Nodding he confirmed Rick's suspicion. The group was stunned to realize that they had not only found a serious stash but a much bigger problem. No one hazarded a guess to the dollar amount of the drugs but they did know it was more then their combined lifetime earnings.

When Becca heard Cole whistling sharp and shrill she dived down at him and mischievously tapped him on the head with a wing tip before gliding and landing behind the bush. She heard his laugh and before he could come hunting her, she quickly changed. She was slipping her shoes on when TJ peeked over the bush to check on her.

She got a look at Becca's knees and gasped. "Holy Hanna, you look like you got ran over by a truck!"

Lacing her shoes, she laughed. "More like a trunk but I'll tell you all about it later." Standing she brushed her jeans off and wished she had worn shorts.

"I heard from the boss you got caught out in the storm. All I can say is that you're damn lucky it landed on your legs and not your head." Shaking her head, she was surprised Becca could walk at all.

"I'm going to keep out of storms from now on, I can assure you!" Smiling she checked the ground making sure she did not leave anything behind before rounding the bush. "I don't want to ever experience that again."

They helped the others load the crates and followed as everyone headed back into town. Becca held on to Cole as they carefully wound their way down the mountain and felt his tension ease the further they got from the meadow. She had to admit she felt a little better knowing the worse part of the day was finally over.

As they finally approached her family's house she wished she didn't have to be there but she had to prepare for tonight. When she slid off the bike, she looked at the house and her waiting mother then back to Cole.

Before she could do or say anything, he grabbed her and gave her a hard kiss, hugging her tightly. "I'll see you later. Get some rest." He growled in her ear as he nuzzled his nose into her hair. "Dream of us and later."

Nodding her head reluctantly, she pulled away and flashed him a grin. "I will, not that it will make the time go any faster." Stepping away, she blushed as thoughts best left to her self raced through her head.

He gave her a knowing wink before waving to Regina, revved the engine, and dropped the clutch, burning a little rubber as he pulled out of the drive.

Becca watched him when he foolishly did a wheelie before turning the corner, disappearing down the street. She couldn't help but laugh at his showing off and hearing her mother yell out he was a darn fool. Seeing her mothers scowl turn towards her, she sobered quickly sure she was going to get a scolding, like when she was seventeen again.

However, she was older now and when she climbed the steps she just grinned. Giving her mother a peck on the cheek, she slipped into the house ignoring the older woman's mumbling about insolence in children these days.

After taking a long shower, she sat at her vanity slowly working on her hair. She had parted it from front to back and was now braiding it into two even plaits, taking her time. When she finished she used an elastic band around the ends to secure them and finished them off with leather thongs wrapped around the bands. Standing she made sure they hung evenly down the front, nodding in satisfaction.

Hearing a soft knock, she opened the door and found her dress hanging from her grandfathers' fingers. "Oh my,' she whispered, stepping back. "Grandda, it's gorgeous."

He stepped in and went to hang it on the closet door. "I had plenty of time to put the finishing touches on the last few days. And,' he paused pulling something from under his arm. "I made you something special."

She gasped at the fan made of hawk feathers, beads and dyed leather. "Oh Grandda, it's beautiful." Taking the gift, she gently opened it and ran a finger over the feathers. Tail feathers of a Red Tailed Hawk made a striking contrast against her dress. The beads went dark, smoky black to light brown on red leather.

She gave an experimental twist of her wrist and she heard the glass beads tinkle as they came together. "I love it, thank you!" Squealing she jumped into his arms and hugged him tightly. "Thank you!"

He chuckled as he held her and shook his head. She was light as a feather and so alive today. "You are welcome child." Letting her down, he stepped back and searched her lit face. "Looks like you're going to be the prettiest girl dancing tonight."

"I wouldn't say that but I will be one of the best dressed." Sighing she looked at her improved dress and had to admit that she was looking forward to wearing it tonight.

"I heard about what you found the other day." He crossed her room and sank on the bed. "I have got to say you've proved you're imaginative. Going back was foolhardy but gutsy as hell." Patting the spot beside him, he smiled. "Let's talk."

Putting the fan on the vanity, she went to sit next to him. "Grandda, I had to do it. It was the right thing to do." Taking his weathered hand, she admitted she was the only one who could have found the drugs without searching for hours if not days.

"I know but you took a big risk yesterday and I just wish you hadn't gone on your own is all." He pushed the fear of losing another grandchild from his mind. "But yes, you did the good and honorable thing." Smiling down at her, he caught the flash of relief cross her face.

She saw his quick frown and felt a lecture coming. "What?"

"Well, I gotta tell ya that it's rather obvious you've become close to Cole again."

She nodded and looked him in the eyes, not bothering to hide the truth. "I love him and if the last few days are any indicator we are a couple again." Rolling her shoulder, she grinned sheepishly. "And we're happy."

"Yes, I saw that yesterday and by the way," he cleared his throat noisily. "You're bruise marks show with your hair like that." He ran a finger over the dark bruises making her squirm. "But it's not completed yet, is it?" Bringing her face up with a finger, he saw her blush. "Why haven't you finished the claiming?"

"Because we keep getting interrupted," grumbling she rolled her eyes dramatically. "You show up then Kyle and there are the drugs. It is as if everything seems to be conspiring against us." Jumping to her feet and throwing her hands up in the air, she huffed. "We haven't had more then a few minutes of peace since the storm and I, I don't know."

Max laughed hard slapping his leg. "Oh child, did you know that your Grandmother and I had to wait six months before we could complete our claiming?"

Grinding her teeth, she snapped her head up and growled at his laughter. "I am not waiting six months. Cole's father wasted four years of our lives already being stupid."

"Grady?" Catching her hand, he frowned. "What did Grady have to do with the two of you?"

Catching her breath she sank to the bed, quietly told her grandfather about his letter, and then showed him the ring. "If Grady hadn't lied we would be married now and we wouldn't have had so much misery."

"Well the past is done and you two have found each other again." Patting her hand, he sighed. "You know what you're going to have to do now, don't you?"

Seeing her puzzled look, he grinned and let her think for a minute. When she shook her head, he took a deep breath. "Well then I suggest you dance with the rest of the unclaimed women tonight along with the story tellers' dance." He grinned mischievously as he rubbed his hands. "Your mother is going to be tickled." Getting to his feet, he caressed her cheek before leaving. "It is just something for you to think about while you're dressing."

She nodded as a slow smile pulled at her lips. Yeah, she thought as a plan began formulating in her mind. The unclaimed women's dance could work to her advantage tonight. It would tell Cole she was ready and it would tell the world that no matter what, they were mates and no one could stop them, ever.

Becca began searching for Cole the minute they arrived in the commons. However she knew they would not get much time together, alone. She saw several friends and waved as they passed by but did not stop to chat.

She thought she had finally spied him by one of the large teepees but quickly realized it was Kyle instead. She nodded when he waved her over and excused herself to her family.

She smiled up to him realizing Cole was not the only Sun Wolf who had aged some in the last four years. However, this one had a short military style haircut and more creases around his eyes. "Kyle, welcome home, belated but welcome!"

Kyle nodded, as he looked her up and down. "You've grown a little Rebecca." His look was cool and a little hard making her self-conscious.

"Yeah, well, I guess I have." She felt a shiver crawl up her back as she became uncomfortable under his gaze. "Where's Cole?"

"He's finishing the last touches on his war paint. Apparently he's taking part in one of the warrior dances."

He shrugged uneasily as he glanced around the throng of people. "Look, I know we never got along that well before but I want you to know I think you and Cole really belong together." He held out his hand and cocked his head flashing the Sun Wolf grin. "Took you two pig heads long enough!" Laughing at the stunned look on her face, he picked her up and gave her a bear hug, squeezing the breath out of her.

Becca squealed and tried to squirm out of his arms. "You are a big obnoxious, jerk!"

He continued to laugh as he released her. "You look good kid, for a runt. I have to tell ya I figured you two were either going to kill each other or wake up and smell the roses." Grinning he pulled a braid like he used to when they were younger. "Clint would be over the moon."

Becca swallowed and nodded. "He is."

Kyle lifted an eyebrow and shook his head a little. "I'd like to hear about that some day."

"Hear about what?" Cole growled as he snuck up behind Becca, grabbing her around the waist. "You two might make people talk the way you're behaving."

Becca squealed again and tried to elbow him in the ribs. "We need to tell him about Clint and the storm." Laying her head back, she wrapped her arms over Cole's enjoying the feeling of him against her.

"Oh, and here I thought he was making a move on my woman." He winked at his brother and grinned.

"She's not my type, trust me." Kyle shifted uncomfortably. "I like my women to be all grown up." He caught her kicking feet and laughed. "As well as a little less feisty."

Becca struggled between them until she was laughing and gasping for air. "Uncle already guys, I give up."

Kyle let her feet go and wisely stepped clear while Cole pulled her back against him.

She shook her finger at Kyle and chuckled. "You'll be surprised when your ideal woman and true mate knock your moccasins right off, Kyle. And I hope I'm there to see it." Turning in Coles arms, she gave him a kiss before everyone who had witnessed their horseplay. She did not even blush when there were a few whistles.

Hearing the drums begin the call to gather she linked arms with the brothers and they made their way to the dance area. She looked up at Cole and smiled as she took in his lightly painted face.

His braided hair was much like hers. However, his braids were tied off with leather thongs and he had eagle feathers hanging from the ends. She caught his eye and winked. When he leaned down, she whispered softly in his ear before blowing in it gently. She could not help but giggle when his eyes darkened and he growled in her ear in return.

She heard Kyle cough discretely and choked back his laugh. "Knock it off you two,' he whispered. "Save it for later when you're alone."

They reached the edge of the corded off dance area and listened as the Elder slash Shaman began the ceremony with a chant of peace and unity. When he had finished, he raised his rattle and Shamans stick to the new moon just beginning to peek over the mountains and the sun began to set at his back.

"We celebrate our lives, our spirits and our families. We celebrate our returned families and we celebrate those who have gone before us. May this celebration bring peace and joy to everyone!" He stepped back as a young man came forward with a lit torch. "May this light show our lost their way home."

When the young warrior laid his torch to the stacked wood, it roared to life making everyone call out, 'La-kee-ha', welcome. The chorus of voices shook the trees and startled the birds from their branches.

Becca saw how tired her grandfather looked and worried a little. She only hoped he would stay for a while tonight and enjoy himself. Turning she saw TJ and Chris threading their way towards her.

She laughed as TJ made a path for Chris, eyeing people warily when they didn't move out of the way fast enough. "Make room folks, let the poor kid breath." She growled more then once as people tried to crowd around him.

Hiding her laugh behind her hand, she watched as Chris rolled his eyes behind TJ's back. She took TJ's hand and admired the other woman's outfit. Breaches and tunic, headband and a single braid down her back made for a simply functional costume and not one bit womanly.

Chris was in a similar outfit but his was more elaborate. He took Becca's hand and smiled carefully. "I wanted to say thanks to you and your mom. I don't think I could've made it without your help." He took a shaky breath and tried to hide his fright. "I owe you my life."

Becca brushed his hair from his eyes and shook her head. "You owe us nothing Chris. And you wouldn't have passed, you're too strong." Giving him a quick hug, she changed the subject. "I heard you're applying to the police academy in Boise this fall. Good luck!"

"Well I'm off to mingle. Chris, no booze and be cool." TJ interrupted as she backed away. She shot him a warning glance and left before they could stop her.

Becca arched a brow at Chris who shrugged back. "Does she ever stand still for more then a minute?"

"Not that I can remember." He watched his cousins' retreating back and sighed. "I love the stuffing out of her but she's been driving me crazy. I can't move without her dogging my every step and nagging at me all the time."

"She worries about her family and friends." Patting his arm hearing her mother call her. Catching Regina's frantic wave she flinched. "Opps, gotta go."

Walking quickly through the crowd she winked back at Cole before she caught up with her mother. Regina waved faster as she stepped into the still empty dance area. "I'm not sure I should be doing this,' she grumbled to her mother as the butterflies began dancing inside her.

"You'll do just fine, you know the story forward and backwards and it's your destiny to be the next Storyteller." Regina eyed her daughter. "You haven't changed your mind, have you?"

"No! I can be Storyteller and do my research anywhere." She wrapped an arm around her mothers' waist and forced herself to smile for the audience. "I'm just nervous is all,' she whispered through her clinched teeth.

They hugged and then separated as the drummers began a low slow rhythm. Regina stepped forward and raised her arms to get everyone's attention. When quiet laid across the crowd she began speaking softly. "I have decided it's time for me to step down as Storyteller." She smiled sadly at the crowds surprise and held a hand out to her daughter. "But we as a people can't go without one. So I'm very pleased to say that Rebecca Red Feather has trained all her life to take my place and she has accepted."

Everyone cheered and several let out shrill whistles including the Sun Wolf brothers who whistled louder and longer. Becca caught Coles wink and knew he understood what her decision meant for them. She was home for good.

When it quieted down Regina turned to her daughter and placed the beaded necklace she had been holding over her daughters bowed head. She placed a gentle kiss on the bowed head and whispered, "knock 'em dead."

Becca silently stood as her mother backed away, closed her eyes and began to sing. The song was loud enough to be heard by everyone but soft enough to tell the story of their beginning.

Everyone was enthralled by her story and there was no other sound in the valley save her voice. As she finished the song, she felt as if she had really brought the telling to life.

When she let the last note fade away, she couldn't see a dry eye and smiled when she saw her grandfather raise a fist over the crowd's heads in pride.

Then the crowd exploded in cheers and a number of whoops from the men. She was instantly surrounded by a group of women, each wanting to be the first to congratulate her and express their gratitude.

She felt Coles hand on the small of her back, slowly helping her to move out of the crowd. She smiled, nodded, shook hands or accepted hugs from the well-wishers. Thankfully, the drummers began a call for dancers and she was finally free to breath. Using her fan she tried to cool off but she really needed something icy cold to drink and mentioned it to Cole.

Cole led her to an empty bench and told her he would get her a glass of iced tea. Before he left, he kissed her hand and winked. "You did great and I'm proud of you."

She felt his pride and whispered, "I love you." Looking around she leaned into him and grumbled. "I didn't realize how hollow the song sounded before when I practiced but now it's real." She shrugged. "I think you know what I'm saying."

"Trust me, I do honey." Kissing her fingers lightly he saw her face glowing with pride and love. Stepping back, he let her fingers slide from his hand. "I'll be right back, don't go anywhere."

She sat back and waved her fan, watching couples as they danced, circling the fire. She waved and chatted with a couple on their way to the food tents. She thanked them again as they left and had to hide behind her fan when she sneezed loudly. Her sneezes lasted for a few heartbeats and she sighed when they abruptly stopped.

"Well, well, well, if it isn't Short Stuff. Heard your performance and it wasn't bad for a short kid." A voice rasped from behind her as it draw near.

She recognized the voice and shuddered inside. "Gee, thanks a lot Miles." She looked over her shoulder and flashed a weak smile. "How's it going?" Taking notice of his dull eyes and Charles Manson face, she hid a gag. His shaggy hair looked unkempt, hanging in his eyes.

"Oh, it could be better but can't complain." He swung over the bench on shaky legs and settled himself in the corner, propping an arm on the backrest as if he was posing.

Swallowing another gag as a light breeze blew from his back, she clamped her lips as a foul odor drifted towards her. "Well, you look like you're doing all right." Granted his clothes were expensive but they were long over due to be washed, as did he. However, she absolutely refused to say he looked good. In addition, he thought he looked like a movie star, she thought to herself.

"Well I've had a few lucky breaks and I'm working on a big deal which could benefit us all." He cocked his head and gave her a wolfish grin, flashing yellowed teeth. "Too bad Clint isn't here to see all this. He would have ate it up and be strutting around like he's cock of the roost."

Becca gasped and looked at her clinched hands suddenly wanting to belt him. She refused to let this jerk see her reaction. She knew there had been a lot of competition between the two but she did not realize Miles had actually hated Clint. "He would have found it interesting," was her only comment.

He slid closer to her, laid a hand on her shoulder taking a deep sniff of the air around her. "I'm sorry, I thought you would be over his dying like that by now." He caressed her with a grimy finger along the side of her neck as if he was trying to stake his claim of her.

She jerked away and hissed at him in warning. "Don't touch me Miles. Moreover, do not try to impress me either. I know you and your slimy, disgusting and evil ways."

"Whoa girl, I'm just trying to be friendly. I said I was sorry about your brother." He reached over to take her hand but stopped short when she changed it. Her hand had raised becoming talons, very sharp and long talons. "Easy baby, I mean no harm."

She slowly changed her hand back as she stood turning her back and she began fanning herself, driving fresh air into her lungs. She only wished she had given him a good cut across his already ugly face. She headed towards the food tents and Cole before she changed her mind.

She barely heard the man when he yelled at her stiff back. "You're still a stuck up bitch Becca, you know that?"

She stopped mid-stride, laughed to the sky before turning, and glared back at him. "Stay away from me Miles. Because the next time you even think about approaching me, I'll have you arrested and locked away for good." Laughing harder at his scowl, she raked her eyes over him as if he was a bug. "And you're still a little worthless creep. Have a good night Miles, I'm sure you'll find some kind of trouble to get into or start." Stomping off she wished she could get the stink of him out of her sinuses. After sneezing a few times she felt a little better, almost running into Cole headfirst.

"Hey, I was coming to you, remember?" He laughed as her tea sloshed dangerously in the plastic cup. He knew she was upset when she grabbed the tea and drank half of it down before taking a breath. "Becca, what's wrong?"

Handing the cup back to him she wiped her mouth with the back of her other hand. "I needed that or I was going to puke." Shuddering she sneezed again.

Cole tossed the cup into the trash and took her by the shoulders shaking her gently when he saw her pale face. "What the hell is wrong? I leave you alone for a few minutes and I find you upset." He looked around wondering if someone had said something to her. "Becca, talk to me please."

"Miles Darkwing happened." Sneezing again, she held a finger under her nose. "Not only has he gotten ballsy enough to approach me, he's filthy, he stinks to high heaven and dared to touch me."

Cole could see that she was visibly shaken and pulled her against him. "He was warned to stay away from you because of your last run in with him. I'm so sorry Becca, I shouldn't have left you alone." He rocked her gently as she breathed him in deeply. "I should have went to the Tribunal myself and demanded they swear out a warrant for him."

He searched the crowd milling around and thought he caught sight of the nuisance but could not be sure. He thought quickly and came up with an idea but first he had to distract her long enough for him to warn Rick that Miles was lurking around. "Hey, let's go see your folks and forget about him. We'll drop a bug in Rick's ear on the way." He tipped her head and grinned. "Maybe we can get in some dances and then sneak out early." Wiggling his eyebrows, he caught her faint giggle. "What do you think?"

She shook her head at his suggestion. "I don't think I can just vanish much as I would love to, Cole. Not tonight and not seeing as I just became Storyteller." Sighing she stepped back and gave him a wink. "But I think we can find a place to hide for a little while."

Chuckling at her suggestive smile, he offered his arm. "May I escort the Storyteller to see the sights?"

Throwing her head back and letting a peal of laughter out, she nodded. Taking his arm, she beamed up to him not hiding her relaxed face. "Good warrior, I would be honored to have such a devilishly handsome and sexy escort as yourself." Hiding behind her fan, she winked at him and licked her lips impishly. Then she sneezed, ruining her teasing. "Damn it. And here I thought I was over it."

Cole frowned and looked at her closely. "Are you coming down with something? You feel okay?"

"I think I'll be okay once I stop sneezing until my head comes off, if I can that is. I have had a few spells like this when…,' Gasping she froze and her eyes went wide. 'When I'm around pot." Whispering she looked around hoping no one was listening. "I'm allergic to cannabis and that entire family of plants."

"Son of a bitch. You were close to Miles and he stank, right?" He searched the crowd again, his eyes dangerously close to changing. He didn't care if there was a celebration going on around them, he was on the hunt now.

"Oh, he stank all right, to high heaven. He hadn't bathed or changed his clothes in days." She shuddered as the image and smells came back to her. "I knew I should have swiped my talons across his ugly face." She growled low and deep.

"Would have served him right." Pulling Becca along, he began searching the crowd for his boss. "We need to find Rick. I have a feeling Miles can lead us to whoever owns the stash or at least tell us how's he's being supplied while he's sitting in a cell."

They found Rick sitting beside his brother at the edge of the dance area pointing out the more enthusiastic dancers. Cole left Becca with Chris and some of their friends while he pulled Rick off to the side. He explained everything in a hushed tone quickly and they agreed to get the other Guardians to join in the search for Miles.

He glanced at Becca while she watched them talking and felt somewhat relaxed when he came back to the bench looking as if he had a secret, squeezing between her and Chris, he was grinning from ear to ear. Rick promised him that him and the other Guardians would handle it as long as Cole kept close to Becca for as long as it took. Throwing his arm along the back of the bench and forced himself to let the tension ease out of him as he ran a finger along the back of her neck. The simple caress was enough to relax him until he was able to enjoy the dancers in front of them.

Becca leaned back, rested her head against his hand, and sighed when he gently massaged the tense muscles. They watched the dancers as they finished the dance and applauded with everyone else. She instinctively knew Cole was hiding something but figured he would tell her if it was important enough so she didn't say anything, just enjoyed his closeness.

When Max's voice called for Mothers to claim their daughters, Becca stood and grinned at Cole with a glint in her eye. She kicked off her moccasins and laughed at his shocked expression.

She stepped towards the now flattened grass as her mother gave a startled cry and ran to her with thrown out arms. She let her mother lead her to the small group gathering around the fire, looking over her shoulder at Cole's still stunned face and gaping mouth.

She took her place in front of her mother, head bowed and arms hanging at her side letting out a slow breath as she steeled herself to do something she swore she would never do. As the slow beat began, she listened as the mothers sang farewell to their girl children and hello to the women before them. As the song slowly built, Becca began to dance, telling her life story, her dreams, her spirits and her empty heart.

As each woman told her story, several young single men stepped forward but did not approach the women as they danced around the fire, building momentum with the drums. They danced around the fire in a slow circle, showing everyone their story.

She saw Cole at each turn of her body, his eyes reflecting the firelight and his own light from inside. He followed her progress with hungry eyes as he moved closer and closer towards the fire and her.

He felt the beat of the drums deep inside him, his heart keeping time and he watched her move as if in slow motion in the fire's glow. He could hear her breathing and he could almost taste her scent in the air. His nostrils flared when he noticed her scent had subtly changed to that musky, heady scent meant only for him.

He didn't realize that he had approached her until the drums stopped with a final loud beat. He stared down at her, seeing her every emotion in her shining eyes, the heaving of her chest as she breathed and the fine sheen of perspiration on her skin. She never looked more beautiful then she did now, standing proudly before him.

She watched him slowly tug the eagle feathers from his braids and slowly presented them to her on his open and trembling hands. She heard the gasps as she took one and wove it into her left braid. When she repeated her actions with the other feather the crowd let out a collective aw. Nodding she mouthed we love you before unwrapping the shorn braid from her wrist. Sliding her shaking hands in to his she pressed it into his palm and smiled up to him with shining eyes.

The crowd began cheering as the couple joined hands and turned to their families gathered behind Cole. Max held a sobbing Regina and nodded to the couple promptly giving their approval of the match.

When Kyle stepped next to Max, clasping the old man's shoulder he asked a private question to which Max nodded. Kyle looked at the couple with hooded eyes and blinked when he saw them surrounded in a soft white light that did not come from the fire. He smiled slowly and gave his own nod of acceptance.

The crowd had held their breath, not knowing if Kyle would permit their union. When it was, they gave a mighty roar in surprise and jubilation. And when the couple kissed, the roar grew louder, echoing off the dark mountains.

The couple relaxed and went to their family for hugs, kisses and handshakes never letting each other's hand free. Becca wiped the tears from her mothers smiling face before wiping her own tears away.

'I should have warned you but I'm glad I didn't." Laughing and crying at the same time, she hugged her mother tightly. "I'm sorry."

"Oh baby, don't be." Regina kissed her daughters' wet cheek. "I'm just so happy for the both of you." She grabbed

Coles face and gave him a resounding smack on the cheek. "Now young man you are truly a member of the family."

"I always was ma'am," chuckling he gave her a hug and a peck on her cheek in return. "I never left." Grabbing Becca's left hand he raised it and showed the ring to his future mother in law. "We just had a mild postponement."

When Regina gave out a squeal they found themselves in her arms again, their faces rained with kisses and more tears.

Kyle stood off to the side a little until they turned to face him, arms crossed over his chest. He cocked his head and squinted at them as they began fidgeted under his stare. "I guess this means I have to put up with her nagging," he grumbled as he ducked his brother's good-natured swing.

"Kyle, are you okay with this?" Becca felt he had reservations and she wanted to know about them now instead of later, when it would be too late.

"I'm fine with it." Taking her shoulders, he grinned down to her. "I always knew you two were meant for each other and it was just a matter of time." Pulling the couple close he gave one of his rare hugs before clearing his throat and pulled away uncomfortably.

Before anyone could say another word the call for the first warriors dance of the night rang out and Cole pulled Becca to the side. "I'm going to do this one dance and I'll be right back." Seeing her slow smile he winked back. "Stay with everyone and enjoy the show."

"I will." Sliding her hand around his neck, she jerked his head down and grinned up to him before pressing her lips to his. "Knock 'em dead." Turning to her family she tried to hide her grin behind her fan but she knew she failed when her mother gave her a knowing look. Turning to the dance area, fanning herself she nodded to Cole as he stepped over the cord, winking again.

The drum beat began in a fast tempo Cole took his place and began the steps he knew by heart. When he looked up to see his 'opponent' he came face to face with his brother and grinned before nodding. As they 'battled' they heard cheers until they threw up their hands when they lost their timing because of laughing too hard and clasped each others arms. Still laughing they left the other dancers to finish the dance while they rejoined the family.

"You could have warned me, bro.' Cole slapped Kyle's back as they stepped over the rope.

"What fun would that have been?" Letting out a rare deep laugh he caught TJ standing there with a raised eyebrow. "Looks like she's itching to participate."

"She would jump at the chance but they won't let her." Grumbling Cole reached out and pulled a willing Becca against him. "She'll get over it."

Becca snapped her fingers under Coles face and nudged him in the ribs. "I think she's itching to get a chance to do the battle dance against Kyle." Snickering she hid behind her fan. "If I remember correctly the two of you had an ongoing competition thing when we were younger."

"She's too tomboyish for my taste these days." Grumbling Kyle stomped to where Max was standing, keeping his back to the couple and the crowd around the dance area.

The couple looked at each other then at his stiff back before looking to where TJ was sneaking looks back over her shoulder. Nudging Cole, she stifled a bark of laughter when Kyle glanced over his shoulder. "I don't think they ever settled that battle, do you?"

Before Cole could answer, Max cleared his throat loudly and jerked his head to the side. "I think it's time we took this someplace more private." Watching the trio, he smiled seeing past problems disappear. "I don't know about any of you but I'm ready to go and have a stiff drink in celebration." Throwing his arms out, he began herding his newly expanded family towards home.

As the brothers' left to get their street clothes, the Red Wolf family accepted congratulations and praises from well-wishers on their way. Becca's eyes never stopped looking for Cole and relaxed when she caught him talking to Rick. She saw his scowl and slow nod before shaking the other man's hand. When he clapped Rick's shoulder, she saw his smile turn into a grin before she began smiling at everyone around her.

He left his brother talking to Rick and ran to her side with his bag. "Sorry, Rick had to say congrats and rib me a bit." He hid part of the conversation from her, not wanting to worry her unnecessarily right now. That was his job as of tonight and for the rest of their lives. It irritated him that no one could find Darkwing lurking around and he was still loose somewhere.

They slowly wound their way through the crowd and when they reached the empty street, Kyle caught up with them. As they made their way to the Red Wolf home, they were laughing and talking stopping once when Kyle inadvertently admitted he was having second thoughts about the union. But he had a hard time keeping a straight face and crumbled under Regina's glare. "Seriously, I want you two to know I want only the best for you. And to be godfather to all the little Red Wolf's to come."

As they entered the house laughing again they didn't even notice the red eyes watching them from under the cover of a bush or its low rumbling growl.

Hours later a weary Becca said a reluctant goodnight to Cole and his slightly buzzed brother telling them to be careful on their way to Kyle's house. She tried to convince them to stay for the night but Cole declined saying it wouldn't be proper. He did however promise to stay at his brothers instead of going all the way to his own home across the valley.

As the brothers slowly weaved their way down the sidewalk, she stifled a giggle behind clamped lips. Cole had his hands full with Kyle tonight as he started baying at the moon, weaving back and forth down the middle of the street. Shaking her head, she closed the door and locked it behind her.

She was bone tired but too wound up to go to bed. She had changed into a calf length skirt and sleeveless blouse when they got to the house but she felt a little chilled. She checked the windows and back door twice before turning out the lights as she slowly climbed up the stairs. She heard nothing but the sounds of sleeping occupants in the other bedrooms as she slowly made her way to her own room.

She undressed in the darkness and slowly pulled her new eagle feathers from her hair. She placed them beside the fan and necklace and ran a finger over one of the feathers. She could tell that they came from Cole's own eagle by the way they felt, vibrating under her fingers in welcome. She had been shocked when he offered them to her but she had not hesitated in accepting them.

Sighing she went to her bed expecting to lay awake for several more hours while her mind raced back and forth over the nights events but she drifted off smiling contently.

Chapter 8

Cole woke to find his grimacing brother shaking him and threw an arm out to push him away. Kicking off the light blanket, he groaned when Kyle tried to shake his shoulder again. "I'm up already." Looking up at his brother, he hid his snicker. "Hell, you look like crap Ky."

"My head hurts but I'm more worried about you man. You have been moaning and groaning for a half hour. It has been loud enough to wake me and the dead." Kyle fell back in the recliner and held his head. "And I was dead to the world too."

"Sorry, I don't remember dreaming." Brushing his hair back, he took a closer look at his laid-back brother. "Got a hangover, don't ya?"

"Humph, more like a hung over. What was that stuff Max gave us anyway?" Kyle rubbed his temples gently and worked his tongue around his mouth. "I remember getting there, having a drink, talking and everything was going along fine. But when we got up to leave it gets real hazy."

Cole got to his feet and padded barefoot to the kitchen and the coffee maker. "He said it was his own recipe and he did warn us that it had a kick to it. I personally think he's got a distillery hidden somewhere in his basement." Pouring two cups of strong coffee, he rejoined his brother, handing him the larger cup. "As to coming home, you howled at the moon and tried to climb a few trees. You're lucky I was there to keep you out of trouble."

He stood at the front window and looked out at the fog that had settled over the village. "I was tempted to shove a sock in your mouth when you started yelling about how you could kick anyone and everyone's ass." He grinned and shook his head. "You're a crazy drunk, Bro. And I hope to hell you don't do it very often."

Kyle sat up slowly and hissed when his head continued to pound. "I don't get drunk Cole, you know that. But I intend to decline any more offers of one drink with that crazy old man."

Cole felt restless and scanned the street again not liking the feeling of his skin crawling on his neck. "I'm going to head over to Becca's. You need to sober up some more and get yourself together." He put his untouched cup on the end table and yanked his shirt off the back of the couch. "We'll catch up with you in a couple of hours, okay?"

Kyle nodded over his coffee and waved his brother off. "I'll take a run once I finish this. I need to sweat that poison out if I'm going to participate in the games."

Cole paused at the door and looked over his shoulder. "I didn't thank you for standing in as my elder last night or for giving us your blessings."

"I did what Pop wouldn't do and couldn't do. You two deserve each other." Kyle nodded at his feet. "But don't mess this up Cole, you'll never get another chance." Turning his head gingerly, he frowned at his brother. "I just want you happy and she's made for you. She's your balance and your other half."

Cole nodded and left before they got mushy on each other. He couldn't handle his brother, the tough Army Special Forces and DEA agent going soft. It was against his very nature, he was a true warrior, not a lover.

As he stepped out into the fog, he had an uneasy feeling that something wasn't quite right and shook off the growl he felt from within his chest. He made the return trip to Becca's house ignoring the damp chill from the fog. He could still smell the smoke from the bonfire lingering and he grinned as he remembered how Becca looked.

She had looked like the white Indian maiden depicted by so many artist's over the years. To him she had looked like an angel in regal dress and her voice was so breathtaking when she had told their first story.

She had blown his mind when she had joined the women's dance, knowing she had always been dead set against that custom. Last night she just jumped in with no hesitation. He had to admit her dancing had been erotic to him if not every other male watching. He remembered glaring at a few of them for their somewhat lewd comments and growling in warning when one of the newcomers tried to step into the area.

He hadn't realized he had stepped forward, taken his feathers off or held them out to her in offering until she took them from his open hands. He only knew that for the first time in his life he had followed his spirits and his own heart. Moreover, he still felt his spirits acceptance of her in every fiber of his body. This was the real deal.

When she had pressed the braid into his hand, he had understood why she had done it. She had found a way to tell him that she was no longer in mourning and she was not going to let it rule her life anymore. He looked down at the braid secured around his left wrist and smiled to him self. She had carefully wrapped it twice around his wrist. She could not help but laugh when there was barely enough left over to tie the ends together.

He reached her house and noticed that there was no sign of activity with in. Checking his watch for the first time since being rousted awake, he groaned at the time. It was barely six and the sun was now only cresting the eastern mountains, trying to burn its way through the fog.

He really didn't want to go back to Kyle's and he didn't want to go home only to turn around and come back. He wanted to see Becca and prove to himself that it was all real, not just a dream. He put his bag on the porch and quietly paced the front of the house, checking his watch as time slowed to a crawl. He was sorely tempted to pound on the door but figured Max would greet him with either a gun or a baseball bat up side his head.

So he took a seat on the swing and began rocking slowly ignoring the slight creaking noise. He could be patient when he had to and now was a good time to practice what he preached.

Becca wished she had waited for the fog to lift before coming to the commons but she wanted to find her moccasins before the dampness ruined them completely. Searching the ground around the dance area where she had kicked them off the night before, she jumped at every little sound. The fog was eerily dense giving her the willies, thinking she saw shadows move and strange noises.

She got to her knees to search under the bench and gave a small sound of triumph when she found one beneath where Cole had been sitting. Clutching the damp moccasin to her chest she was about to get up but she heard a pair of voices approaching.

"This had better be damn important for you to get me up this early in the morning." A deep voice growled in the fog. "And if it's another one of your sick delusions I'll smear your face all over that tree."

"I swear this is important man." Miles whined and sniffed noisily. "Last night I went up to check on our investment after I made a few good sales."

"Big deal," The voice huffed. "How much of the goods did you sample while you were making the deals?"

Becca covered her mouth as she hunkered down making her self as small as possible, not believing she was overhearing this! Moving slowly she slid to her stomach and wiggled under the bench praying she wouldn't get caught. She couldn't leave unless she wanted to be discovered and in an uncomfortable position.

"Not enough to ruin a good night. Besides, the boss doesn't mind if I make sure we're selling quality stuff."

"That's up for debate," growled the other voice. "Let's get on with why you woke me up."

"All right, all ready. I went up to check on the goods but when I got there the only thing I found was empty holes." Miles hissed, pacing behind the bench. "It's all gone, everything is gone."

"What do you mean it's gone?" The voice moved closer and Becca heard a scuffle. "If you're bull shitting me I swear I'm going to rip your head off, you little weasel."

"I swear to God, every bag is missing. Some one dug them up and took it all!" Miles screeched.

Becca caught a whiff of Miles as he moved around and almost sneezed. Slapping her hand over her mouth and nose, she opened her eyes only to see two shadows facing each other.

"Do you know what the boss is going to do to you if this is true? You had better find that stuff and fast, if you value your skin. The boss is going to fillet you alive as an example to everyone else." The deeper voice moved and cuffed Miles upside the head. "And you know I'm the one who'll have to dump your miserable carcass like so much garbage."

"I'll find it, just give me some time. That is all I'm asking. I'll find it and get it back, all of it." Stepping back Miles bumped into the bench rocking it. "Just don't tell the boss for a day or two, okay?"

"I'm giving you one day to find it, Miles. And you're the one who's going to break the news, not me." The bigger man stepped closer to Miles and poked him hard in the chest. "I've kept my hands relatively clean in all of this and I'm not going to jeopardize my life for your screw ups." Stepping back, he waved the air and fog in front of him. "And for god's sake, take a shower and change your clothes. You stink to high heaven, no wonder the women here run from ya."

"Sure thing man, anything you say. Just do not breathe a word of this to the boss. Please?"

She heard the whining tone coming from Miles and guessed that this boss whoever he was had Miles scared silly.

"One day Darkwing, no more." The bigger man stepped back into the fog giving a final warning. "Stay away from the booze, the women and the drugs, Miles. If there are any more complaints, the boss is going to let you start hanging. Boss is fed up with your crap and you can be replaced by some one who's more competent."

Becca had to swallow her snort and bumped her head on the seat of the bench. Freezing where she was she held her breath when both men jumped.

"What the hell was that?" Miles hissed, spinning in a circle.

"I think we had better leave. Just remember what I said, punk." the bigger man moved quickly, letting the fog swallow him. "You have until sunset tomorrow, Miles."

"Yeah, yeah," Miles mumbled as he leaned against the bench. "One of these days big man, you're going to get yours." Punching the backrest, he gave a disgusting sniff before making a rude sound. "Lay off the drugs, my ass."

Becca laid her head down slowly watching Miles's shadow as he paced the length of the bench. She tried to ignore the wet grass soaking through her shirt and pants but it was uncomfortable as hell. Trying not to shiver was nerve racking and smelling Miles as he paced was turning her stomach.

She couldn't believe that he could smell worse then he did last night but he did. Watching him without moving her head she wished he would just leave so she could get the hell out of here and tell Cole what she had just overheard.

She wondered if there had been any busts last night and if anyone had narced on Miles for being a seller. If so then the Guardians would be looking for him and they would get him before his boss found out about the missing drugs.

Watching him start to walk away, she moved slowly out from under the bench, careful not to make any noise until she knew he was gone.

Sitting on the bench she shivered as the realization of what she had overheard meant. Miles was working for someone who was ruthless, who didn't care about his or her people and who would stop at nothing to get what they wanted. Trying to put a face to the other voice, she came up with a blank, which frustrated her to no end.

Seeing the fog begin to lift she heard someone else approach and felt Cole coming up behind her. Turning towards him, she took a shuddering breath before jumping up and running to him. "Oh God, Cole," Crying she launched herself into his arms. "They know the drugs are gone."

"How do you know?" Holding her close he felt her shaking and looked around.

"I overheard Miles and another man talking. I was under the bench hiding and they were close." Burrowing into his arms, she clung to him. "Miles found the holes last night after selling a bunch of his drugs."

"Easy Becca, start from the beginning." Stepping back, he noticed she was soaking wet and decided she could tell him once they got to her house. She did not need to catch a chill standing out here. "Let's get you home first then you can tell me about it."

"That's fine with me. I don't want to be seen anywhere near here right now."

Once at her house Cole called Rick and asked when he was going to be in the office because they needed to talk to him. Hearing that Rick was already in, Cole promised to be there shortly after extracting a promise from his boss that all of the Senior Guardians would be present. It was better that Becca only tell what she overheard once then have to repeat it, upsetting her more.

Becca came down shortly after showering and changing but she looked as if she was having second thoughts, chewing her lip nervously.

"Hey, you did the right thing Becca." Taking her hand, he kissed the ring before tucking her trembling hand in the crook of his arm. "I won't let anything happen."

"I'll be okay. Just a little nervous, I guess." Shrugging she fell into step with him. "It seems that I've become a magnet for trouble lately the way I stumble into things."

"A good magnet, one that only sees and hears. At least you haven't stepped into a situation." Patting her hand, he opened the door for her. "I can feel your pull still."

"Cole!" Slapping his arm with her free hand, she gave him a nervous laugh. "How can you think like that now?"

"Sorry. Just saying what I feel. Besides, that's the first smile you've given me today."

"Hmm, I'm going to have to remember to withhold all bad news until I've smiled, I guess."

"No, don't ever do that. I would rather get hit with the bad so that we can clear it up to finish the day on a good note." Nudging her shoulder, he squinted up to the sun. "We have plenty of time to fill everyone in and still make most of the games today that is if you still want to go."

"I don't know." Chewing her lip, she looked around. "Let's see what you and your group comes up with first."

"I can live with that."

After Becca told everyone in the conference room what she had overheard she spent another hour answering questions until she threw up her hands. "Look, I don't know who the other one was, I never heard who the boss was and I don't know anything else." Raising her voice with each statement she finally had enough.

"Becca." Cole warned her gently when he felt a slight draft in the enclosed room. "It's okay."

"I'm sorry guys. I'm not used to being grilled like this." Ducking her head, she folded her hands on the table taking a deep breath to calm herself and get a grip on her rolling emotions. "I have some questions of my own, if you don't mind."

"Go for it." Rick nodded watching her compose herself quickly. "Maybe it'll spark something with these guys."

"Were there any drug related arrests last night?"

"None, why?"

"Well if there had been there would've been solid proof against Miles and he could've been arrested. What I've told you is considered only circumstantial, right?" Looking around the room, she saw several nods. "Another question is how come Miles gets off so easily when he's caught breaking the law?"

Seeing a few shrugs, she raised an eyebrow. "Look, I'm not a Guardian by a long shot nor am I looking to become one but shouldn't someone be checking in to this?"

"We never thought about Miles being involved in the drugs, we just knew he was a royal pain in the ass. We knew he was using occasionally, but never thought he was smart enough to be dealing." TJ shrugged looking a little sheepish. "But you can bet we'll be watching out for him more earnestly from now on until he's caught."

"And I'm going to assign either Christie or TJ as your escort until we nail him. They know how to not make it look too obvious so no one will be the wiser." Rick leaned on the table his hands folded before him. "For Cole, your family and my peace of mind."

"Thank you but no." Standing she shook her head in refusal. "He doesn't know I'm involved in any way and if you do that, he'll know. I'd rather go on as normal as possible, if you don't mind."

"Becca, please." Cole whispered clasping her arm. "Just think about it."

"Cole, I refuse cower for doing the right thing. I'm stronger now and I can defend myself." Standing her ground, she looked around the room leveling everyone with a determined glare. "I'm not going to let him scare me or let him get away with this. I've done my job, now it's your turn." Walking to the door, she smiled back at the stun faces around the table sweetly. "I no longer need a babysitter."

Leaving the room, she started counting and reached two before Cole came running after her.

"Becca, you are a stubborn woman, you know that?" Growling he grabbed her arm and gently swung her around. "Reconsider."

"Only if you're assigned as my guard." Grinning she patted his hand. "We've made our intentions clear last night and everyone will expect us to be inseparable now."

"You're not only a stubborn woman, you're also devious on top of it." Chuckling he pulled her back towards the conference room. "Let's tell Rick before he assigns shadows for you."

"He wouldn't." Gasping she frowned up to him. "Would he?"

"In a heart beat." Chucking her chin, he grinned back down at her as he led her into the conference room. Opening the door Cole nodded to Rick and heard the collective sigh of relief from everyone around the table. Seeing TJ's arched brow he shrugged. "Looks like she knows who the better man is."

"Oh ha, ha." TJ jerked her nose up in the air. "She might reconsider when I beat you at the games today."

"Whoa, if the two of you are at war I don't want to know about it." Becca laughed as the two scowled at each other.

Everyone in the room laughed and the tension in the room dissipated. Rick howled as TJ stood and leaned over the table, hand extended out towards Cole. "I'm game."

"You're on." Cole smirked as he pumped the woman's hand. "Tomahawk, archery and foot race."

"Throw in spear chucking and you're on!" TJ laughed richly. "I still owe you for the last time you beat me by an inch."

"Ha, it was six inches and you only lost because you cheated."

Rick started coughing and slapped the table. "Enough all ready!" Nodding to Becca, he tried to keep a straight face. "These two have been in a competition since Cole came back."

"I see. Well, hopefully they'll get it out of their systems." She answered, eyeing the two as they kept up their silent battle. "I would hate to see a man beat a woman in these games. We woman are just as good if not better then the male warriors." Winking at TJ, she clamped her lips together to keep from laughing. "I just hope he's up to making dinner for the winner."

"All right, that's enough." Cole growled as everyone started howling with laughter again. "Becca, who do you want to be with you while the Jar head and I are battling because I don't want you alone."

"Well since I'm doing this under duress I think Rick would have to do." Wrinkling her nose at him, she softened her facial features and realized she needed to be serious. "I trust you above everyone else other then Cole of course."

"I would be honored to stand at attendance with the new Storyteller." Sobering Rick stood and looked around the room. "Becca, we all want you safe and you're being the Storyteller is one of the biggest reasons you're safety is important, I hope you know that."

"I understand. I'll be honest, I had forgotten about my new station." Cringing she had the decency to blush. "I'm sorry if I've been difficult." Looking around she nodded to each person in apology.

"We understand." TJ grinned and returned the nod. "Boss, we done here?"

Rick nodded and went to shake hands with Becca. "Games start in an hour."

"We'll be there."

Standing on the sidelines during the foot races, Becca cheered the racers on until she was almost hoarse. She couldn't decide who she really wanted to win, Cole or TJ so she cheered for both of them. Grabbing Rick's arm she jumped up and down when the pair ran past her, neck and neck. When Cole crossed the line by only a breath, she gave one final squeal that made Rick cringe. Laughing she hugged him before slipping through the crowd to catch up with Cole.

Feeling a hand on her shoulder, she spun around to come face to face with TJ. "Hey, good race!"

"And where do you think you're going?" She huffed as she bent over trying to catch her breath.

"I was on my way to congratulate Cole." Looking around she searched for Cole and caught a glimpse of him making his way to her. Waving she jumped up and down. "And here comes the victor."

"And I'm gone." TJ stepped back snarling. "Next time Sun Wolf, I will beat you." Holding her hand out, she shrugged sheepishly. "Next time I'll get some sleep before the race."

"Hey TJ, you gave me a damn good run for my money." Taking her hand, he smiled at Becca. "And next time I'll make sure you have the night off before."

"Gee thanks, Cole. Remember that next time you make out the roaster if you can. Almost a month of nights is a killer." Punching him in the shoulder, she grinned and turned to leave. "By the way, she tried to go looking for you without Rick."

"TJ!" Becca gasped seeing Coles scowl. "It's not like I was running away or anything. Besides, you know who isn't anywhere to be found."

"Becca,' Cole warned. "We talked about this."

"I saw no harm in it!" Hissing she glanced around.

"All right you two,' TJ laughed stepping between them. "You're starting to make a scene so kiss and make up, fast"

Becca bit her lips together and looked up at Cole trying not to laugh.

"Becca, we'll discuss this again later.' he growled before sweeping her into his arms and bending her backwards. "It's a good thing I love you too much to paddle your bottom." Kissing her deeply he raised his thumb to the cheering crowd.

Becca clutched at his shoulders not hearing the crowd only the pounding of their hearts. When he finally broke the kiss, she realized they had a large audience and hid her face in his shoulder. Feeling Cole's deep laugh she began to giggle and pulled away to face the crowd. "To the victor go the spoils."

Before anyone knew it the call for the next event was announced and the crowd slowly broke up leaving the couple standing there facing each other. Cole took her left hand and kissed the ring she wore. "Please, be careful, Becca."

Nodding, she slid her arm around his waist. "I will, I promise." Letting him lead her to the next set of games, she quietly teased him about almost losing to TJ. "She gave you a run for your money and I thought she had you there towards the end."

"I thought so too but when I heard you screaming I got my second wind." Ducking his head, he whispered. "I've heard you scream like that before."

"Cole Sun Wolf!" Slapping his chest, she felt her cheeks redden. "I never scream."

"Oh yeah, you do and I'll prove it to you, later." Growling in her ear, he let out a wicked chuckle. "All night long."

"Stop it!"

Reaching the improvised ring, they found two young men facing each other about to start their wrestling match. Cole paused long enough to see who was in the match and then lead Becca over to his brother and Rick.

"When are we up?"

"You're up next and I go after. There are ten matches and then we start the double eliminations." Kyle never took his eyes off the wrestlers as he leaning back, giving his brother a half grin. "Wanna place a bet this year?"

"I'll put my money on TJ." Rick grumbled as he wiggled a finger in his left ear. "Then again, if you two wind up going head to head I have to bet on Cole."

"TJ gets disqualified every year, you know that." Cole laughed, eyeing his boss. "Something wrong with your ear, Chief?"

"Nothing that some peace and quiet won't fix." Not taking his eyes from the ring, he smirked. "Banshee Becca almost broke my ear drum."

"Oh Rick, I'm sorry!" Becca moved to face him. "Does it hurt badly?"

"Nah, just lost a small percentage of my hearing for the next day or so." Rubbing his ear, he shrugged. "I've lived with TJ and CJ, remember. Those two were worse then anything I've ever heard."

"Still,' she paused until she saw the twinkle in his eye. "Oh you old fraud!"

Tweaking his nose, she giggled. "You're lucky that was my happy scream, my angry scream is worse."

"She has different screams for different emotions?" Rick shuddered as he stepped away from her. "Heaven help us."

"She can do worse then scream, trust me." Cole grinned rubbing his cheek. "She can pack quite a wallop when she wants."

"Cole." Becca warned quietly. "Let's not go there."

"Yes ma'am." Cole held up his hands in feigned fear. "Just don't hurt me."

Hearing the crowd cheer, they turned their attention to the ring to see one of the opponents being pinned. After the count of three, the winner jumped up and held his hand out to the man on the ground. When the downed man took the offered hand, the crowd went wild at the show of good sportsmanship.

Hearing Coles name called out, he turned to Kyle and jerked his head to Becca. "Keep her out of trouble, would ya?" Turning to Becca, he raised an eyebrow, "And you will remember your promise, won't you?"

"I'll be good." Nodding she grinned back sheepishly. "Be careful."

"Always." Giving her a quick kiss, he turned and went to the ring. Stepping over the rope, he peeled off his shirt and tossed it to Becca with a wink.

Becca held his shirt tightly against her chest and held her breath when she saw his opponent. Mike was at least thirty pound heavier and had almost six inches in height on Cole and he looked mean. Feeling a nudge on the shoulder, she turned to see Rick's wink. "I don't like this."

"Those two are good friends and they wouldn't hurt each other intentionally. Relax."

"I'll try." Taking a deep breath, she tried to relax but couldn't when Mike charged Cole when the referee dropped his hand. Burying her face in Cole's shirt, she moaned when she heard the crowd gasp. Peeking up she saw that Cole held Mike's arm and Mike was kneeling on the ground. Swinging her eyes to Kyle, she saw him nodding in approval and relaxed. Cole knew what he was doing and he was proving to be the better wrestler.

When Cole finally let Mike go, they were facing each other grinning as if they were ready to go at it for real, Becca had to excuse herself. Seeing Kyle's scowl she nodded towards the Facilities, eyes wide. Mouthing she would be right back, she stepped back to leave.

"If you're not back in five minutes, I'll send someone after you." He called to her back. "And I'll tell him it was too much for ya!"

"Jerk!" She called over her shoulder tossing Cole's shirt over her shoulder knowing he would, just to make her squirm.

When she was finished, she took a quick look at her reflection in the polished metal that served as a mirror and sighed. At least no one expected her to look her very best on a day like today. Shrugging she turned to see a mother with her young child enter. "Nice day."

"Oh Storyteller, it's the best!" The mother prodded her child to the closest stall. "We've had so much fun."

"I'm happy to hear it. How are you settling in?"

"We're settled and getting comfortable with being able to be ourselves for once. Tell the Elder thank you for helping us, will you?" Checking on her child, she beamed and whispered. "We're on day two of no accidents."

"That's great!" Patting the woman's shoulder, she stepped towards the door. "Enjoy the day!" Letting the door close behind her she smiled when she heard the mother praise her child and wondered what it would be like to do that her self one day. Sitting on a nearby bench in the shade, she took a deep breath and just looked around.

When the mother and child left, she heard the mother tell the child that that pretty woman was the new Storyteller and she was special. Seeing the child look back at her in awe, she waved and smiled at the round-eyed child.

Closing her eyes for a moment she sat back and listened to the cheering crowd knowing she did not have much time left before someone came looking for her.

Suddenly feeling as if she wasn't alone, she looked back and saw Miles standing behind her, arms crossed over his chest with a smug look on his face.

"Looking for something Becca?" He shook his hand, dangling her other moccasin from his grimy finger.

"Oh, you found it!" She flashed a quick smile of gratitude and forced her stomach to be calm as she stood slowly. "I totally forgot them last night when we left, too much excitement I guess." Walking around the bench, she held her hand out for the item and frowned when he held it up where she couldn't reach. "Miles, I would like my moccasin back. Please?" Jumping up to snatch it, he jerked it back over his head.

"I tell you what, I'll give you your little slipper and your missing backpack if you tell me where you hid our drugs." He stepped closer towards her, scowling. "I've got a lot invested in that stuff and I have to have it back. NOW!"

She saw the look of pure rage in his bloodshot eyes along with the dirt, leaves and pine needles covering his clothes. He looked like he had rolled on the ground after taking a mud bath. Glancing around quickly she wished to hell there were some people around.

"I don't know what you are talking about." She tried to step away from him but he pinned her against the back of the bench with his body. "Miles, give me the damn moccasin. I already told you I don't know what the hell you're talking about." She pushed at him with all her strength but he grabbed a handful of her loose hair and jerked her against him. He pulled her head back and let his eyes glow as he raised his fist.

She swallowed back a cry and held her breath waiting for him to strike at her. She squeezed her eyes tight and let a soft cry escape her lips. "Miles, please. I don't know what you are talking about, I swear."

"You are such a liar, Becca,' he growled, shaking her by her hair. "I went up to the tree line last night and guess what I found. Holes, empty holes. I went back again today and could smell everyone who had been there, especially you. Your scent was everywhere and I happened to come across your little bag a ways away." He shook her again. "Now, you are going to either tell me where it is or you show me because if you don't you can be assured I'll do more then just hurt you."

"I don't know where it is! Honestly Miles, I don't know." She gasped, refusing to let him see her cry. "Rick and the Guardians took it and locked it away. I wasn't with them after they took it, I went home." She glared up at him refusing to mention Cole.

"Oh, there's one thing you left out Becca. You forgot to mention your lover and his bad ass brother. They stank up the place with their stinks." He pushed her back but held on to her hair. "You stink of him." Bringing her hair up to his nose, he inhaled deeply. "You've been claimed by him,' he sneered. "A little odd considering how he was practically to blame for your brother's murder."

She did not contain her anger and slapped his face, crying out. "Cole had nothing to do with Clint's death. Faulty equipment was to blame." She felt her anger override her fear and she refused to cower before him.

"Yeah, so I've been told. Too bad he didn't check his d rings and harness before taking that climb." Miles hissed pulling up on her hair harder. "He always was so gung ho and righteous. He had a real bad habit of sticking his nose in everyone else's business."

Becca stared at him in disbelief. "What do you know about Clint's death?" She whispered as chilling shudder passed through her. "You knew the equipment was faulty, didn't you?"

"Hell, I should hope so. I didn't have a lot of time to make every thing look accidental. I actually took a great deal of pleasure following those orders. I just wish Cole would've made the climb too." He let an evil laugh out, enjoying the emotions flashing across her face. "But watching Clint fall and Cole finding him was a kick. I never thought Cole could scream like that, just like a girl."

Chapter 9

Becca could not hold in her anger any longer and gave a loud cry as she tried to swing at him with her fists. He moved quicker then she expected and grabbed her by the throat cutting off another cry and her air.

"I don't think you want to be with your precious brother right now. What would happen to your family and Cole?" He warned as he slowly squeezed. "Behave yourself bitch or I'll put you down like a rabid dog."

She gasped and choked as a tear slid from the corner of her eye. "I'll kill you, you bastard."

He threw back his head and laughed. "Not if I don't kill you first." He leaned into her bringing his face within an inch of her face. "Now, we're going to get my drugs and then we'll see what my boss wants to do with you." Turning her roughly by the hair, he pushed her ahead of him. "Don't try anything cute, Red Feather or I'll just have to shoot you. And no changing either, a bullet has a devastating effect on a spirit animal." He threatened, poking her in the back.

Stumbling, she clutched her moccasin to her chest and began walking. She didn't know if he really had a gun or not but she wasn't going to try to found out. She had to play along and figure out what she was going to do to get out of this mess. "Where are you taking me, Miles?" Keeping her voice calm, she hoped she could get through to him. "People are going to see us and they'll wonder what is going on."

He just grunted and pushed her harder. "Keep going." He kept sweeping the area for onlookers but the ongoing games seemed to be to holding everyone's attention, for now anyway.

She tripped over a rock and fell, crying out when she landed on another. Miles landed almost on top of her pushing the rock deeper into her stomach. As she struggled against him, she felt his hand hit her face hard enough for her to see stars dancing before her eyes.

He jerked her into a sitting position and pointed his gun at her forehead tipping her head back. "I won't tell you again, walk, don't talk or I'll shoot you."

She nodded slowly, eyes wide as she scooted back a little. "Okay, you win Miles."

As he got off her, she slowly got to her knees and stood on shaky legs. Her head ached, her face burned and she felt as if she was going to be sick.

He nudged her forward again but did not move to grab her just in case someone happened to see them. They were just two people walking around looking at the different games.

When they reached the edge of the village, he had her turn south, heading for Boyd's Lake. She knew that no one lived near the lake and she began to panic. No one knew where she was and wouldn't know she was missing for a little while yet.

When they reached the lake, he had her go east, keeping to the tree line where no one could possibly see or hear them. Her panic grew the further they went and she was helpless to do anything about it.

He started talking once he was sure they were alone. She thought it was nerves at first, but when he lit a joint, she knew he was coming down from drugs and needed a pick me up. When he blew the smoke at her, he had a fit of giggles when she started sneezing.

"What's the matter Becca? You don't like weed?" He blew more smoke in her face, watching her eyes water and she sneezed harder.

"I'm allergic to pot!" She gagged and turned her head to avoid inhaling the blue smoke. She needed clean air to clear her head more then anything right now. She realized she still held her moccasin so when she bent over sneezing she let it slip quietly out of her fingers. She just hoped someone would go in search of her and be able to track her scent, finding the moccasin and rescue her. She could only hope and pray it happened quickly.

As they began climbing the eastern mountains, she felt sweat began to trickle down her back as the sun rose higher. She paused long enough to pull her flannel shirt off and tied it to her waist. Her sleeveless t-shirt was sticking to her back and she pulled it from her skin trying to catch a breeze.

Miles wouldn't stop talking about how he was helping his boss by running drugs and trying to get people on their side to allow the logging. The chatter never slowed and Becca began to ask questions.

"So Miles, who's this all might boss of yours? He must be pretty smart to run an operation this good without getting caught." She peeked at him from the corner of her eye, hoping to glean some information she could use later, if there was a later..

"Oh the boss is real smart and there's no one who can figure out what we're up to." He boasted mopping the sweat from his face. "The boss has gotten all of this figured out and planned for problems. We run drugs after harvest, get new customers when the logging starts and we make a fortune." He laughed pushing her forward. "Everyone gets rich off of the lumber contract and the boss gets richer off the drugs we're going to sell. This is where you come in." Grabbing her arm, he swung her around and pointed the gun at her. "I think you had better start talking little girl."

She stepped back, holding her hands out. "Miles, I told you the Guardians took them away. I don't know where they took them, I wasn't told." She almost went to her knees but her pride kept her standing proudly in front of him. "You have to believe me, Miles. I don't lie."

"Just cut the crap, lady." He snarled as his eyes shifted back and forth. "You tell lies just like us normal, little people only yours are bigger and better."

"I don't lie, Miles. I don't know how." She dragged her fingers through her hair pulling out several strands. She then held her hands out, fingers spread wide to let the hair float away. "I have no reason to lie to you. You're the one with the gun."

Shaking his head, he tried to focus on what she was saying to him. "Don't matter anyway. I will just have to make them a deal, you for the drugs. It's the only way,' he mumbled almost to himself. "They can't refuse. The new Storyteller can't be harmed." He suddenly became aware of their surroundings and waved his gun. "Get a move on. We've got a little more to go before we can rest."

Becca nodded and started climbing again but she was getting tired and clumsy. After skinning her still tender knees for the third time, she broke down and begged for a break. His only answer was to scream at her and started dragging her by the arm. She fought back but his drug-hazed mind didn't hear her and she stopped struggling, trying to keep her feet beneath her. When he watched the weaving path before him she reached down and slowly untied her shirt, letting it fall on to the rocks.

When the sun was well over the mountains, he called a break, pushing her to the ground at his feet. He mopped the sweat from his face with his grimy shirt and licked his dry lips before cursing the building heat.

She sat there limply and looked down the mountainside hoping against hope that someone was coming. Pulling her hair over her shoulder, she began combing it out with her fingers letting the strands fall to the ground as she went. She then knotted her hair to keep it from snagging in the tree limbs. Wiping her sweaty hands on the dry grass, she let her scent permeate everything she touched.

"Enough. We've wasted too much time already." He jumped off the rock and pulled her up roughly. Pointing to an outcrop of rocks above them, he pushed her forward.

Cole watched Becca as she stumbled, baring his teeth at Miles when he kept pushing her forward. He had been tracking them along with his brother since they had realized she was no longer by the restroom facilities.

When he had finished his match, he turned to look for Becca but she was nowhere in the crowd. Seeing his brother scowling, he ran over and looked at the spot Kyle was staring. His shirt lay on a patch of trampled grass just beside a bench and the restrooms.

Hunkering down Cole sniffed deeply. "She was here all right and not too long ago." He picked up the shirt and smelt her scent faint but there, mingled with his own scent. Taking another deeper sniff, he blocked out their scents and caught a rank odor on the collar. "Son of a bitch. Miles was here too and he had his hand on this." Cole looked up at his brother, scowling. "He wouldn't be smart enough to keep away from her after she threatened him." He looked the grass over and could see where she had kicked a patch loose. He didn't see Kyle kneel to his right but felt his hand on his arm.

He looked where Kyle silently pointed and he saw some blood, mixed with the dried grass. He felt his stomach sink as he touched it, bringing some of the damp grass to his sensitive nose. "It's Becca's,' growling, he closed his eyes. "She's scared and angry as hell."

Turning to his brother he didn't hide his rage. "The son of a bitch took her." Standing he looked more closely at the grass and could see faint foot prints, heading east. "I'm going after her and I'm going to kill Darkwing this time. Are you up to it?"

Kyle gave him a chilling grin and nodded solemnly. "I'll take to the sky. It's been a while since I was on a real hunt." Ripping off his shirt, he grinned, throwing the shirt on the nearest bench. "Keep your head Cole. We don't know what Darkwing is up to or capable of doing to her."

Cole nodded as he followed his brother's lead. It only took a few seconds to change, Cole into the wolf to do the tracking and Kyle into the eagle for the air reconnaissance. It didn't take long for them to catch up, thanks to Cole's keen senses. Miles rank odor was heavy in the air and it was on every thing he had touched. Becca's scent was deeply implanted in his person that he could have found her trail after months of being there.

He crouched behind a bush while an eagle soared over their heads, looking as if it was just riding the air currants. However, he knew his brother and he wasn't only tracking them, he was looking for a way for them to get around Darkwing.

Kyle dipped and turned lazily as he saw the man and woman climb toward a cliff and he realized they didn't have much time to plan. Screaming he dove, banking away from them, and heading towards the valley again.

Cole knew his brother would find a safe place to land, change and be joining him shortly. He didn't have to wait long as he felt another wolf approach silently behind him. "And?" he growled softly turning his head but not his eyes.

"They're headed for that cliff which is a dead end. There's an old trail that runs above them but it is dicey going." Kyle shook himself before hunkering down. "Our only chance is going to have to be a surprise attack. The wind will be at our backs but I think if we keep to the sage and bitter brush we'll be okay."

Cole nodded and slowly stood, not sure if he was ready to face another part of his past. He knew that trail well enough and he knew that cliff, too. He had been avoiding it ever since he came home. The last time he had been there he had held Clint in his arms and cried out his anguish. It almost seemed as if history was trying to repeat it's self. However, this time it concerned his mate not his blood brother.

Shaking his great head, he turned to his brother. "We had better move. I've been watching Miles and he's starting to get a little edgy." Jumping out from under the bushes, he ran for the beginning of the old path with Kyle hot on his tail.

They got close at one point and heard Miles as he screamed at Becca to move faster. Cole gave a low deep rumble when Becca cried out that her knees hurt too badly to move any faster. He felt the fur on his hackles rise and was getting ready to jump over the rocks but Kyle grabbed him by the scruff of his neck growling. He bared his teeth at his brother but Kyle wouldn't let go until he calmed down.

"If we make our move now he'll shoot her as sure as I'm standing here. They were almost there and then we can make our move, not one minute before. You can take frontal attack while I come in from behind. He's freaking out and that's to our advantage."

Cole nodded and shook his body, gathering strength from his surroundings and his brother's good sense. "Let's go, I don't want to know she's getting hurt worse then she already is."

They split up before they reached the cliff and Cole waited until he knew Kyle was in position. He had been watching Becca and he thought at one time that she caught his scent, smiling to herself. However, she kept calm moving with a little more ease and confidence.

She looked out the corner of her eye and caught the flash of a black wolf before it disappeared behind some rocks and turned her head to hide her grin. Cole had found her and it wouldn't be long until she was safe.

Hearing a small rock skitter and bounce down the cliff ahead of them before it rolled off the path, she caught sight of another black wolf as it ducked into some thick bushes. She let out an involuntary gasp knowing that this wolf could only be Kyle ahead of them, waiting for his chance. She had seen that wicked grin enough times to know that he was enjoying the hunt a little too much.

Miles swore and jerked her arm harder as he continued to drag her behind him oblivious to what was happening around them. "If you don't keep up I'm going to drop you off this cliff by your hair! I'm not going to tell you again!"

She shuddered at the tone of madness in his voice and tried to keep her balance as she scrambled over the fallen tree lying across the path. "You're going to do it any way Miles." Panting she dug in her heels, yanking her arm free. "You already know where your stupid drugs are so you don't need me anymore."

"You're right but you know too much and I haven't figured out what I should do with you yet. Besides, I need to talk to the boss and report what you've done." Grabbing her hair, he pulled her against him, forcing her head back. "I might even get to keep you for a while." He ran his tongue across her cheek, enjoying her look of repulsion. "Maybe I'll plant my seed in your belly and let you go." Rubbing his hand over her stomach, he licked his lips and smirked. "I don't think Sun Wolf would have you after you've given birth to my bastard."

She didn't think twice just reacted by bringing her head up and head butted him as hard as she could, right on the nose. He released her as he grabbed at his broken nose, howling in pain and feeling blood pouring through his fingers. She heard the gun clatter to the ground and then it fired. The bullet ricochet off the rocks beside them scattering rock chips around them. She made a mad scramble past him, ducking under his waving free hand as he continued to howl.

Reaching the smaller cliff face, tripping over fallen tree limbs, roots and rocks she desperately looked for a place to hide. She spied the small opening of a long forgotten cave and scrambled in before he caught up to her. She heard him stumble, cursing her and held her breath when she saw him standing at the opening of the cave, blocking her only escape route. She was inside, trapped and the only way to get her freedom was to fight her way out.

Shedding her clothes in the cramped cave quietly, she quickly shifted into her eagle giving her more room to move easily. She saw him turn and kneel, peering in with dilating, spiritless eyes. "Looks like you've gotten yourself trapped, Becca. Don't make me come in there after you." Reaching in, he tried to grab at her but his arm reach was a few inches short when she moved back.

She flattened herself against the rough side wall when he bent lower reaching further in and when his hand got too close, she bit him. Her strong pointed beak broke through the skin and broke bones as she clamped down, refusing to release him. As he jerked his hand, she bit down harder, feeling his blood begin to pour from the bite wound.

She could taste of all the drugs and booze that he had been using to pollute his system for so long and realized that it all had changed him beyond being a shifter.

She hissed in anger when he finally broke free and began beating at the entrance causing earth and rocks to loosen and rain down on her. He was trying to cause a cave in, burying her alive inside. She began to panic and let out a piercing scream that echoed inside and out as she threw herself to the back wall.

Cole couldn't wait any longer, not knowing what was happening on the other side of the rock pile. When he heard that scream, it felt as if a knife had ripped through him cutting his heart in two. Jumping from the rocks, he gave a howl that would have raised the hair on a werewolf's back.

Kyle echoed his brother as he jumped from behind the bushes down to the cliff shelf.

Cole took some satisfaction when Miles fell back and found himself laying between two very large and very pissed off, black wolves. He watched the man as he swung his eyes between them and swallowing convulsively. As he took a step forward, he let the pale man see his bared teeth and growled loudly. By the second step, he was nose to nose with Miles and smelt the distinct odor of fresh urine.

Sitting down he just stared at the man, daring him to make a sudden or threatening move. Kyle sat on the other side of Miles and sniffed the air, shaking his head in disgust.

The prone man slowly sat up and cautiously wiped the blood from his nose, making sure he didn't give them the idea he was going to fight. His other hand was a mangled mess and he kept it tucked under his good arm.

The wolves looked at each other for a moment and Cole nodded as he backed away. Circling around the man, he kept one eye on him and the other on the cave entrance. When he heard Becca scrambling around, he ran to the fallen dirt and began digging. When he heard frantic movements, he dug faster sending dirt flying out behind him. He cleared an opening big enough for her to get out avoiding the loosened earth caused by Miles. He was greeted with a cry of joy as her hands pushed more debris out of the cramped space in front of her.

As she crawled out, she took several deep breaths and wiped Miles's blood from her mouth with the back of her hand. "I thought I was going to be buried alive in there," she whispered to Cole as she hugged him to her breast. "He's lost it, Cole. And he's spiritless now."

He leaned into her, listening to her pounding heart knowing she wasn't seriously hurt. Hearing her warning he nodded, understanding that Miles Darkwing was beyond help now and more dangerous. He knew the stories of what happened when a Shifter lost it's spirit, irreversible madness.

Kyle turned his head for a moment to see that she was out and safe but he didn't see the knife flash before it sunk deep into his shoulder.

Cole moved away from Becca at his brother's howl and jumped at Miles before he could stab Kyle again. As they rolled away from the wounded wolf, Cole heard Becca's cry of concern but kept his attention on the man scrambling to his feet, the knife in his good hand.

Becca moved to go to help Kyle only to see Miles leap at her, landing between her and the other wolves. Ducking under his grasping wounded hand, she felt a rush of air across her back towards Miles.

Cole knocked Miles to his back, his paws on his shoulders and began snarling and snapping in the prone man's face. "Don't. Touch. My. Mate."

Crawling to Kyle, she heard a scream and looked up to see Miles swing his knife at Cole, crying at him to watch out. Cole clamped his jaws around Miles wrist and they wrestled until Miles released the knife, letting it clatter to the ground a few feet away. With a savage kick to Coles ribs Miles broke free and crawled back, hissing as his hands found nothing but air under him. Rolling to his side before he fell over he began laughing madly. "You want the bitch, you can have her."

Scrambling to his feet, he glared at her before realizing there were now three wolves standing before him. The black brothers flanked his sides while a very large, shimmering silver ghost of a wolf stood before him.

Becca saw the silver ghost appear in front of her between the brothers and took an involuntary step towards it, her shaky hand held out. She stopped when it turned its great head, blinking its gold eyes at her.

"Clint," she gasped as she fell to her knees. Seeing its head dip she cried and held her hands over her heart. "Oh Gods."

The three wolves stared at the man as he stood before them gasping for breath through his gaping mouth. They caught the look of panic when Becca called her brothers name and he started to shake violently. They stepped closer, acting as one, surrounding him with only a few feet between them.

Becca stood where she had been kneeling, not making another move afraid that Clint would disappear again. She heard Miles's groan and heard wolves return growl. Their growls grew until they were so deep that the ground vibrated with them.

"I killed you Clint!" Miles screamed madly. "I watched you fall. You're dead, you're not real!" He shook his head, squeezing his eyes shut hoping the ghost would go away. "I killed you, I killed you." He covered his head with his arms trying to deny what he was seeing.

"Why?" The silver wolfs deep rolling voice echoed through the mountains eerily. "Why did you kill me Miles? We were friends." It stepped forward and cocked it head at the shaking man.

Miles took a step back, suddenly laughing hysterically. "We were never friends. I despised you the first time I laid eyes on you and when you started getting nosey about my business, I did what I was told to do. I took you out of the picture before you could discover our budding drug operation." Miles pointed a shaky finger at him and sobered a little. "You were getting in our way and you brought it on yourself." Taking another small step back, his heels hung over the cliff edge.

The wolves didn't move, knowing if they did, he would either fall or jump before he could finish his confession.

"I put a file to some of your gear and cut at your harness's to make it look like equipment failure and it worked. I only wish Sun Wolf would have made the climb with you!" He laughed madly as he looked at them, his face showing signs of sudden rage. "I told the boss all about it afterwards and the boss decided that we needed to tone down the operation for a while." He glared at Becca, his eyes taking on the look of madness again. "We were doing fine until that bitch found our biggest stash." Screaming he jumped towards her but he was instantly blocked by the three faster wolves.

Cole snapped at his wildly reaching hand and growled menacingly. "I told you to never touch my mate." Jumping at Miles when he tried to move at Becca, Cole went for the kill this time aiming for his throat.

Becca jumped back against the rocks as the wolves began tearing at the mad screaming man. The screams mixed with the growls and snapping teeth, grew louder as the echoes bounced off the rocks around them. She crouched down and covered her ears to block out the worst sounds of the battle but couldn't tear her eyes away.

Before anyone realized it, Miles kicked at the silver wolf and screamed in frustration when his foot sliced through air, losing his balance. Becca saw him waving his arms in slow motion as he fell backwards over the edge. His final scream died when his body landed on the rocks below, making a sickening sound.

Becca screamed when she saw one of the brothers collapse at the edge, not sure which one it was. As she ran to the fallen wolf, she recognized it was Kyle, still bleeding from his shoulder wound. She saw the blood flowing down his leg to the ground and matting the fur. Quickly pressing her hands over the wound she prayed she wasn't too late. She felt Cole come up behind her, change and didn't flinch when he knelt just to her side resting his hand on her shoulder. Leaning against him, she felt his racing heart and his heaving chest. "We need to move him back a little,' she whispered softly, feeling Kyle panting heavily.

They carefully lifted and moved him away from the edge as gently as they could, ignoring his repeated growls of pain and warning. Becca looked around desperately for something to use as a pressure bandage but saw nothing usable.

When her brother's ghost stepped to the other side of the fallen wolf, he nosed her hand away from the still bleeding wound. She hadn't felt his touch but she did feel a gentle pressure pushing at her hand. She saw his love for her in his glowing eyes before he turned his attention to the injured.

Cole watched his brother closely and saw the wound suddenly stop bleeding and the slashed skin slowly pull together, knitting to itself. He brought his head up to see Clint smiling at him and swallowed. "Thank you, brother."

Clint nodded as he stepped back, letting Kyle rise awkwardly.

Becca felt Clint pulling away and reach out a hand for him, letting a tear fall. "Don't go Clint, please."

He shook his head sadly, as he slowly began to walk backwards. "I've pointed you two to the right path. I can do no more and I've finally found my peace." he nodded to Cole and Kyle. "It's your battle now, my friends. Finish it before it's too late." He turned to Becca and sighed softly.

"Your job is to tell our stories, old and new. You are the one who has to keep our spirits alive. I know you'll do our people proud." He rose on his hind legs and slowly changed to his human form smiling gently as he stood before them. He looked across the valley sadly before walking away with his spirits at his side. Looking back over his shoulder into Becca's shimmering eyes, he silently spoke to her heart.

She nodded slowly and laughed as she wrapped her arms around Cole. "I promise, we will," she whispered snuggling into Cole's chest. "I love you too."

Before anyone could move, Clint walked away, calling a final message over his shoulder. "Be happy my family and remember me." Little by little they faded away on a light breeze.

Cole looked into Becca's sparkling eyes and raised an eyebrow at her. "What did he tell you?"

Smiling tenderly she shook her head. "I'll tell you later."

With the two wolves escorting her, they reached the village a few hours later to find that the entire Guardian force was in an uproar at their sudden disappearance. They had realized that something was wrong when Kyle hadn't appear for his wrestling match and Rick went in search for them. He found the brothers clothes near the facilities and he found the small patch of Becca's blood on the grass.

He immediately called in all the Guardians and began a thorough sweep of the area for them and for Miles Darkwing. When the trio finally reached the village Rick didn't know if he wanted to throttle them or to throw his arms around them. After being delivered safely to her family Becca took a few minutes to get cleaned up as the men got their cloths and changed before they made their report to Rick personally.

Cole stood behind Becca as she gave her rendition of what had happened up to the point where the men confronted Miles, never letting go of her hand. They sat in the dinning area of her families' home refusing to go to the Guardian Office when she was asked to come down and make her report.

The three of them had omitted the parts about Clint's ghost, saying that Miles had boasted until he realized he had incriminated himself. They stuck to their story that Miles had jumped from the cliff, committing suicide instead of giving up his boss's name and to keep from being punished, when Rick asked them repeatedly.

Rick took them back to the bottom of the cliff and only shot them a puzzled look when he saw the markings of fangs and claws across the man's body. Raising his eyes at the unmistakable evidence of fang marks on Miles throat he just scratched his scalp. "Looks like he put up one hell of a fight,' was his only comment as he turned the deceased mans head and closed his eyes.

No one said it but everyone knew that by a fluke of nature, Miles Darkwing had landed on the exact spot that Clint Red Feather had four and a half years ago with his neck broken. Becca and Cole could only look at each other and hold on to the knowledge that Clint found his peace. Miles had died as his first victim had except his death wouldn't be mourned.

Kyle looked up the cliff and rolled his stiff shoulder, his face expressionless as he searched for an answer. He kept his thoughts to himself as they finally left the attendants to claim Miles's body. He grumbled quietly that they should have left it there to rot as a warning to others before stepping away.

He thought he saw a brown wolf looking down at them but wasn't sure until it turned its back and slowly faded. Turning to his brother, he realized that Miles's spirit had forsaken him forever with no hope of salvation.

Becca laid a hand on his arm as her and Cole moved to leave. "It's the way of the spirit, Kyle. Don't question it, just believe."

"There's a lot that I didn't believe until today." Grumbling he patted her hand and walked beside the couple. "I might not ever accept it."

By the time the dust finally settled, the trio had returned to the Red Wolf home, where everyone could tell the Shaman the untold parts of the day's events. They were tired and relieved to be able to tell someone about Clint and his part in the demise of Miles Darkwing.

Cole finally admitted that he had a dream of Clint and that he had hinted at his death actually being murder. He then admitted that he was supposed to have died that fateful day as well. He felt Becca shudder in his arms and held her closer as he told the family that he had found his damaged climbing gear. He then went on to tell them that he convinced Rick to send in his equipment along with Clint's, to be properly examined by the state forensics lab. Shaking his head, he realized that he didn't have to worry about the results anymore, they had finally gotten the truth.

Seeing his brothers odd look he cocked his head. "I know it's hard for you to understand all of this but it really happened. You saw Clint, you fought beside him and you felt him heal you."

"I know." Scrubbing his face, he tried to come to grips with his first encounter with a spiritual being. "It's just hard to digest."

"But you believe, don't you?" The Shaman asked quietly. "You've never had a moment of déjà vu or a dream that came true?"

"No, I never have." Shaking his head slowly he turned to look out the window. "I'm not sure I want to either for that matter."

Becca caught her grandfathers look of concern and knew he was planning to do a little magic when Kyle least expected it. Smiling to her self, she winked at him when he looked back at the couple.

Kyle left shortly after assuring everyone that he was fine, though there was now an ugly red scar on his shoulder. Cole had hid his laugh when Regina fussed over his brother until she finally gave in when Kyle growled out a promise, swearing up and down he would go to the clinic in the morning.

Chapter 10

Two days later when everything finally settled down to normalcy, Becca packed all of her belongings into the back of her truck. She refused to listen to her mothers pleas to stay, even stood in front of her, plugging her ears at one time. She took a few minutes to look around Clint's room and realized for the first time that her family had emptied it out years ago. Hearing her mother returning she left the doorway and steeled herself for another bout of pleading and tears.

She finally threw up her hands in frustration after ten minutes and snapped at her mother. "For goodness sake mom, I'm only moving to the other side of the valley! It's not like I'm running away again." She took her mothers hands and held them against her heart, begging her silently to understand. "I belong with Cole and nothing you can say will change my mind."

Regina shed another tear as her lips quivered and nodded sadly. "You're right but why can't you wait until you've had a real wedding? It'll only take us a few weeks to arrange everything."

"Because we already had one, Mom. We had a simple exchange of vows with the sun and moon as our witnesses last night. We don't need nor want all the pomp and circumstance, especially with the way things have been lately." She looked at the Black Hills Gold band fashioned into encircled wings that Cole had commissioned years ago. "It's our life Mom and enough time has been wasted."

Stepping back, she squeezed her mother's fingers before letting them go. "It's what we want." Turning her back to the stunned look on Regina's face, she picked up the last packed box and calmly walked out of the house to her truck.

Pulling the truck door open, she smiled brightly at her grandfather and paused to look around. "I still expect to see Clint come running out of the house laughing." Shaking her head, she climbed into the cab and slammed the door over her mothers renewed protests. Starting the engine, she waved, pulled out of the drive and went home.

As she drove, she thought about last night and smiled to herself.

They had left her family right after dinner and raced up to the meadow hand in hand, before the sun began to sink behind the mountains. Laughing they knelt in the center of the meadow, facing each other until they caught their breaths. Before long, they were staring into each other's eyes and interlocking their fingers as the peace of their surrounds soaked in.

Cole must have felt the moment was right because he released her left hand and dug into his pocket for the ring he had been carrying with him for years. Slipping the ring on her finger, he took a deep breath and looked up to the sky. "Becca,' clearing his throat full of emotion, he tried again. "Rebecca, you are the missing piece of me. You fill my life where it has been empty, with light, hope and love.

My spirits claim your's as their mates and now I claim you as my wife."

Becca held back the tears but seeing the beautiful aura around him grow she took a jagged breath letting one fall. Taking the ring her mother had given to her father when they married from her pocket with trembling fingers she smiled. "Cole, you have always been there for me though at times I couldn't see it. Your love never diminished through our lives in good times and the bad times. You let me walk on my own and never used your love to possess my spirits or me. As my spirits have claimed you as their mates, I now claim you as my husband." Slipping the ring on with her shaking hand, she looked up to him and whispered. "For ever and always."

Standing as one they faced the only two witnesses of their exchanged vows and kissed for the first time as a united couple.

Cole heard her pull up the lane and waited for her to stop the truck before he pulled her out and into his arms. "Took you long enough," he growled before kissing her soundly. "You said you wouldn't be longer then two hours and it's been almost four." Picking her up, he swung her around until she wrapped her legs around his bare waist squealing in delight.

She held him tightly and laughed at his antics between the kisses she placed all over his face. When he finally stopped spinning, she leaned back, locking her hands behind his neck and grinned. "I would have been back in two hours except my mother started in about a proper courting period and a wedding in a few weeks." Shaking her head, she wrinkled her nose. "What have you been doing since I've been gone?"

Holding her by her hips, he sat her on the hood of his truck and stood between her knees. "I went and talked to Rick for a little bit. I've got the next few days off to spend with my new wife and while I was down there I learned some strange news." Rubbing her knees, he looked up and took a deep breath. "No one is willing to stand in attendance at Miles's burial and the council won't let him be buried on our land. They hope the message will deter others."

Catching her breath, she now understood her grandfather's vehement refusal of her attending the emergency meeting yesterday. "I can understand their ruling. But for him to be without attendants is strange."

"Not as strange as an anonymous person paying for the cremation and funeral." Leaning down he laid his forehead against hers. "They think it was his boss, but no one remembers who or when the money was paid. So we're still back to square one."

Reaching up she ran her fingers through his hair and gently kneaded his tightening neck muscles. "You and the Guardians will get him when the time is right." Whispering she brought her lips up and gently kissed his. "I just know you will."

Sliding his hands along her bare legs, he slowly inched the skirt of her sundress up over her knees. seeing her eyes widen and then soften he gave her a lopsided grin. "How much trouble can we get into in a few days?"

"More then we can handle, I think." Whispering she scooted closer and pulled him into her with her legs. "But finish telling me about what you've been doing first."

Taking a deep breath, he tried to ignore her hands as they slowly slid across his chest and back. "I signed the owner's deed for the rental over to Kyle, he deserves and needs it more then I do. And I did a little work in the house."

Clearing his throat, he stilled her wandering hands in his. "That's about it."

"And what are your plans for the rest of the day?" Whispering she nuzzled his neck before nipping at it. "Anything I can help with?"

Pulling her off the truck by her hips, he pressed himself against her and leered down at her. "I think we can come up with something to work on." Growling he lifted her up easily and held her by the waist above his head.

"So what's the hold up here?' she breathed softly in his ear as she bent over him letting him see the growing hunger in her soft eyes. "Bring me home Cole."

They entered the house and Cole kicked the door close with a resounding thud without breaking the breath-stealing kiss she had started. He slowly let her slide down his body and pulled away from her reluctantly. He had a plan and if he wasn't careful, she would distract him from it, ruining everything.

Whispering for her to close her eyes he turned her around little by little and pulled her back against his chest. Telling her to open her eyes, he smiled.

Becca looked at the living room and gasped at the changes he had made. All of the furniture was haphazardly pushed against the wall and a small crackling fire was burning in the fireplace. Candles lay scattered around the floor encircling a makeshift bed covered in rose petals and ferns. She sighed as Cole wrapped his arms around her and leaned back in to his chest.

She surrendered to his feather light, searching lips and hands as he slowly slid her sundress up her body. When she was free, she arched her back and moved her arms up circling his neck, locking her hands under his hair. Pulling his head down to her neck again she silently told him she couldn't wait any longer.

She groaned softly as his hands roamed her body, finding the secret places that he only knew of. When his fingers found their target, she gasped as he slowly worked her body towards the proverbial pinnacle of the mountaintop. She felt her body grind back against his in time with his finger and his growing response pushing against her back. The increasing movements of his finger and his hips made her dance, driving him harder.

She felt the heat inside her growing, expanding until it filled every fiber of her being consuming her. She fought to keep the explosion from happening, wanting to make the feeling last. She started making small cries and gasped when he gently squeezed her breast with his free hand. When he slowly sank his teeth in to her shoulder, she lost the battle and cried out. Her ears began to ring with her cries of release and she felt as if her body was exploding into a million brilliant little stars.

He held her tightly against him as she convulsed and cried, tears scalding his arms. He could taste the intensity of her orgasm, her essence rolled across his tongue becoming a permanent part of him. He could hear her repeating his name joyously, over and over in her mind, before she gave one last convulsion and collapsed in his arms.

He slowly released her shoulder, feeling as if he had finally filled all the empty places in himself with her. Picking her up in his arms, he carried her to the pile of thick quilts and gently laid her down. Brushing her hair away from her relaxed face, he saw her beauty shining brightly. Amazed by the tears still flowing down her face, he kissed her closed eyes, tasting the tears of joy and release mingled with her scent, becoming a part of her unique and special signature.

Becca slowly felt her self come together piece by piece, as she drifted back to earth and took a deep slow breath. Fluttering her eyes open, she saw him leaning over her, staring at her with amazement and his never ending love in his eyes. Reaching up she ran a finger along his jaw and cleared her throat. "I never knew it was like that. I didn't feel that when your eagle staked his claim of me four years ago."

"He only staked his claim, this time both of them claimed you at the same time." Whispering he lay beside her, tucking her head under his chin. "Everyone says that it's special but I think spiritual is more like it, especially when there's two spirits."

She looked up and watched the flutter of his beating heart in his throat several times, fascinated by the movement. She reached up, put a light finger on it and felt the flutter strengthen. She turned to her side facing him, touching him with feather light fingers down his chest, exploring him everywhere. She could hear the low rumble and felt it vibrate through her fingers encouraging her to explore more.

Moving her fingers slowly down his body, she felt his stomach muscles tighten at her touch and she could see she was causing more then his abs to tighten. Catching her bottom lip between her teeth she stared in to his eyes as she carefully loosened his suddenly too tight jeans letting her nails scrap across the denim. She caught the flash in his eyes, gave him a slow sexy smile as she ran a finger under the waistband and brushed a nail over the sensitive skin.

When he flinched and gasped, she let out a soft giggle and moved her hands to his hips, slowly pushing his jeans down, freeing him at last. She slid herself down his body until her hands reached his thighs and then began pressing her lips on his stomach, following her hands.

Once she tossed his jeans away, she felt his urgency in his grasping hands and she didn't waste any more time. She crawled up his legs, never breaking their eye contact until she held him in her small hand and slowly lowered herself on to him. He was big and she took her time letting herself adjust until she couldn't take anymore. Rotating her hips, she laid her head back and let out a small cry when he gave a small jerk and slid in a little further, filling her more.

She felt his hands guiding her hips as he began to match her movements and she heard his low sounds, echoing her own small sighs. Building a steady rhythm the only sounds that could be heard was their sounds of pleasure and their heavy breathing. Becca felt the building of her orgasm and gasped when it became to be too much for her. "I can't take anymore."

He sat up, keeping her locked against him by sliding his hands to her bottom and pulled her closer, making her groan when he brushed against a nipple with his lips. She arched her back and cried out when he gently tugged the hardened nub, scrapping his teeth across the sensitive skin.

She wrapped her legs around his waist as a small shudder washed through her feeling his erection brush against the nerve endings inside. When she felt the blankets against her back, she whimpered as he slowly withdrew from her but sighed when she felt him reposition himself. When he slid back in he threw his head back and growled as he sunk in further then before as she tightened her muscles clasping at him hungrily.

She felt his hot breath against her temple, felt his arms pressing against her sides and his hands cupping her bottom pulling her up to meet him.

His movements came fast, hard and she felt him expanding more, pushing her once more to that summit. She became wild, clawing at his back and lightly nipping at his shoulder. She felt her muscles tighten more around him and found the pressure building to the point of being almost unbearable. She felt him drive himself in one more time and bit his shoulder as he called out her name.

Her own cry was muffled against his skin, as she tasted him on her tongue, filling her with his scent and his love for her. In an instant, she saw and felt everything in him that made him the man he was now. She felt his loneliness through the years, his many fears and the elation of knowing she now belonged to him, heart, soul and spirits. She slowly released him panting, sweat and tears running down the sides of her head.

She now knew him better, down to his deepest core, where his dreams, his fears and his spirits resided. She had seen them watching her, loving her and welcoming her home.

Lying before the fire Becca watched the low flames and smiled when Cole told her how he thought her dancing reminded him of those flames as he caressed her hip and back. Resting her chin on his chest, she watched the flames reflect in his eyes as he spoke. She wondered if he ever thought of becoming a Storyteller or even a writer, the way his words seemed to come to life.

"Hey, are you falling asleep on me?"

"No, just thinking." Turning her head, she thought she saw a silver flash above the flames and smiled softly. "I've got something to tell you."

"Hmm, let me guess, you're hungry?" Grinning he pulled her closer and kissed the top of her head.

"No, it's about a promise I made a few days ago." Wiggling until he released her, she grinned and climbed over him, sitting on his stomach. "Remember just before Clint left, I said 'I promise, we will' ?"

Getting to his elbows, he watched her face as it began to glow. "Yeah, I was a little jealous because he had a special message just for you."

Shaking her head, she leaned closer and kissed him. "The message was for both of us."

"It was meant for us?" Pulling her down and holding her tight, he rolled until she lay under him, pinning her to the blanket with his body. "What did he say?"

"He asked us to name him after him." Whispering softly she watched his eyes as they began to change colors as confusion crossed his face.

"Who's him?" Leaning down he nuzzled her neck and then realized what she was saying. "Clint wants us to name, . ."

"Yes, I promised we would name our son," She caught her breath when his head popped up and she saw the biggest grin she had ever seen on his face. "Our son after him."

"Our son!" Laughing he looked down at her flat stomach and back up to her. "Now?"

"Well, it's possible but I think he meant when and if the baby comes." Giggling she chewed the inside of her cheek. "You're not mad I made the promise?"

"Hell no!" Laughing he caressed her face and shook his head. "Our son, Clint." Staring at her, he envisioned a child with her eyes and his facial features, toddling to the door to greet him after a day at work. He also saw his son and himself playing catch in the back yard as she rocked their newborn daughter in her arms. Grinning he imagined a house full of their children, proof of their love.

"Cole?" Waving her hand before his stunned face, she claimed his attention. "Earth to Cole."

"Huh? Oh, sorry." Looking down he caught her slow smile and her feather light touch. "Becca," sighing out her name he gathered her to him and surrendered to her touches. "We'll have to work hard to fulfill that promise, won't we?"

Reaching for his lips she sighed, "Every chance we get, Cole. Every chance we get."

About the Author

Born and raised in Wisconsin I entertained my family with stories, never imagining I had taken the first step towards a fantastic journey. I've written a few short stories and they are patiently waiting to be revisited.

This series, The Guardian Saga has been a labor of love since I started, all starting with a gift from my husband. A dreamcatcher necklace woke the writing gears and it's been full steam ahead since. I've laughed, cried and rejoiced with my characters hoping I've done them justice though none have complained as of yet. Before you ask, no the gears haven't slowed down and I don't think they ever will! There are more characters clammering to come out and it will be interesting to see how they develope on paper. I hope you enjoy the Guardians as much as I did writing!